For Scales Alone
Daniel Sheley

Ashwake Press

Contents

Chapter 1

Smoke in the Warrens

The tunnels sweated with salt and life. Stone here was never dry; it breathed with the sea, wept with it. Fissures exhaled tide-warm air that curled along the floor, carrying the hush of waves muffled by tons of rock. Every wall bore the record of claws—scratches layered over scratches, generations of small hands turning seabed into shelter. Smoke still clung to the ceiling. The warrens smelled of brine, singed rope, and the faint copper of scale-oil.

Morning meant rhythm, not sun. A hundred chores rose together: cooks banked coals with palms black as the pans; fish split clean under knives of sharpened bone; hatchlings skittered until a hiss sent them upright like proper folk, little claws ticking stone, tails twitching to keep balance. A hammerstone tapped leather somewhere down the main run—tap, turn, tap—steady as a second heart. A pair of elders shuffled by with nets over their shoulders, nodding toward Jed's niche before vanishing into the side shaft.

Jed sat cross-legged in his stitch-niche, tail curled thick around his ankle, awl in one hand and a bone needle in the other. It was scarred from work, the tip blunted from years of scraping stone floors. He was stocky for his kind, broad-jawed, scales the dull gray of wet stone. His claws were worn smooth by thread, his shoulders carrying a quiet hunch, like someone who had learned not to expect ceilings to be kind.

Opposite him, Kep—three seasons old and restless as a dropped ember—twitched and kicked while Jed tried to finish his slipper. The boy's pale tail lashed happily against the wall, slim and quick like the rest of him.

"Hold still, or I'll stitch it to your foot," Jed muttered, tightening his grip on the boy's ankle.

Kep snorted a laugh and kicked again, his tail thumping the wall, pleased with himself.

"You kick one more time, you'll wear thread burns for a week." Jed didn't look up, though his mouth quirked. He bent and pressed his muzzle briefly to the boy's heel before setting the needle steady again.

At the mouth of the niche, Yarra sat plaiting net twine. Her scales were burnished copper, catching the dim with a warm edge. She was lean, sharp-frilled, her brow-crest giving strangers the impression she was always scowling. Her tail was long, the frill at its tip flicking when she was impatient. She glanced at her husband with dry humor.

"Threatening him before first meal?" she said.

"Not a threat. Promise," Jed said.

"If he kicks wrong, you'll put the awl through him," Yarra said, not looking up. "You've seen it before."

Jed said nothing, but his grip tightened.

The slipper came out neat. Kep stared at it like the tunnels themselves had bent to gift him magic, then smacked it proudly against the stone. A pair of hatchlings passing by stopped to giggle, only to scatter when an elder hissed at them to mind their steps.

First meal was salt fish shaved thin, algae cakes that hissed in a pan black with history, and a wedge of kelp bread scavenged from Grayhaven's trash heaps. Yarra tore hers in half and shoved the bigger piece at Jed.

"Eat. You're working yourself thin."

"I sit all day," Jed said.

"You bleed thread all day," Yarra shot back, the corner of her mouth twitching.

"Thread's mean!" Kep announced through a full mouth, crumbs spraying.

Jed tapped the boy's tail with his own. "Chew slower. If you choke, I'm not cutting it out for you."

Kep's eyes went wide. "You would!"

"Try me."

Yarra smacked Jed on the shoulder with the back of her hand, but her laugh carried down the tunnel. A neighbor across the way called for quiet, and Yarra called back something sharp that made the woman chuckle before returning to her nets.

Later, they passed the mark-stone at the bend where rock had split ages ago. Every family's cut lived there: spirals, hash-marks, crude signs depending on the patience of the cutter. Jed's was simple—one line with two short cuts through it, a tiny door. He'd carved it the day Yarra tied red thread around his wrist and called him hers, making her not just his wife but his bond-mate.

Inside it, smaller and new, was Kep's mark. The boy pressed his small hand against the stone, pale scales glinting.

"That's ours, right? All of it?"

Jed laid his broad hand over the boy's. "Ours." He fished a sliver of leather from his pouch and tied it around Kep's wrist. "A stitch. For luck."

"Luck's for people who plan badly," Yarra called, hauling a coil of nets past. Her grin softened the words.

The day's rhythm carried them to evening. Songs rose to keep breath steady in tight places. Names were counted—hatchlings new, elders gone to the tide—because numbers could tame grief, if only a little.

Kep fought sleep until he lost. Jed tucked an old net under the boy so he wouldn't roll off the shelf, brushing a knuckle along his brow. The child's tail flicked once and went still.

Yarra hefted three nets across her back. "If the tide is kind—"

"—it never is," Jed finished.

"Then we'll be kinder."

They started up the south shaft, hands finding old holds in the stone. The air thinned, cooled. Salt came sharp. Another smell drifted with it—smoke, but wrong.

Jed paused, nostrils flaring. Not kitchen smoke. Not sea-coal. Something harsher.

Yarra's frill twitched. "Could be a fish fire," she said quietly. "Could be someone foolish with kindling."

Jed's hackles prickled. "Could be dogs."

They held each other's gaze for a moment, both knowing the rules of their life: don't borrow trouble, but don't ignore it either.

Far above, the faintest echo reached them—a sound out of place in the breathing rock. A bark. Short, sharp, answered by another.

Jed's hand found Yarra's wrist. She didn't tremble. "Back," she said, steady.

Chapter 2

The Attack

The first dogs came as sound and smell. Jed heard the cloth-tear bark, bay, snap—trained throats hunting. He smelled wet fur and tar pitch riding the stone throat. Beneath it, men.

Yarra froze. Jed's hand found hers and squeezed. Small bones, strong. No tremble. "Back," she said.

They slid. Knuckles skinned, claws sparking. By the mark-stone bend, the warrens were already changing shape.

No screams. Breath saved for work. Hatchlings pressed flat between adults and wall, tails looped tight. Elders lifted—hand under elbow, shoulder under hip. Scales rasped scales. Buckets of sand passed hand to hand. Hearths were smothered. Guards caught up spears, strung crossbows with oily cord, eyes already measuring the chokepoints.

"South shaft," Jed told Hesk, who for once had stopped rehearsing his death. "South is bad," Hesk rasped. "West is worse. Go."

Yarra cut through bodies like a blade. Jed kept one hand at her back, the other warding elbows. The warrens had always held them. Tonight they pressed too tight.

A boot struck stone above—iron at the toe. Too heavy for watchmen. Too certain. "Pitch," a voice said. "On the captain's mark," another answered.

Smoke came low and mean. Not the damp coal smoke they knew. This crawled—thick, biting—the stench of tar stuffed in pots and rolled alight. Jed hated not already being at the shelf to shield Kep.

They found him there, pebble-puzzle clenched so hard the stones cut his palm. "Up," Yarra said, steady as stone. She bound him to her chest in netting. "Hold. Don't kick." Kep kicked once anyway, then locked still, muzzle tucked under her jaw.

They moved with the current toward the south throat. Smoke followed, hunting. Dogs' claws ticked closer. Guards braced spears in the narrow. A crossbow twanged; a cry choked short.

At the bend, the first mercenary appeared. Chain-and-leather bulk filled the tunnel. A matted wolf-hide draped his shoulders. Beard thick, sweat-damp. Scar ridges across his knuckles. His eyes half-lidded, bored, as if this were habit. Men pressed behind him, shield rims scraping stone. Dogs slid low, ribs showing, muzzles stained.

"They stink of fish," one muttered over his shield. "Work's work," another replied, flat. "Captain says clear the holes, we clear the holes," a third said.

The name drifted with the smoke—Veynar. Jed caught it like a spark.

The spear line broke in the rush. Dogs low, men high. Shields ate points. Weight did the rest.

"Go!" Jed barked. He shoved Yarra ahead, claws scraping. "I'll keep them off." She shoved him back instead—hard—into a side crawl. His shoulder cracked stone. Kep squealed once before Yarra's palm covered his muzzle. Jed dragged them deeper until the rock pinched his hips.

The smoke found them there. It had fingers. It closed. "Down," Yarra said. They pressed bellies flat, muzzles to damp stone. Kep's chest hammered against her ribs. Jed counted heartbeats until numbers slipped.

Then the roof groaned. Not men—stone. The shelf above split, dropped in one breath.

Jed threw his arm over Yarra's head. When the settling came, he was on the wrong side of a wall that had never been there. He dug because stopping meant admitting.

6

Claws split, bled. He levered with his awl until the handle snapped. He pressed his muzzle to cracks and found none. He said their names until they broke in his mouth. Then he set his brow to stone and let out an old kobold sound he had not made since he was a whelp. It ripped, failed, died.

He found a crawlspace and circled back.

The main run was gone. The mark-stone lay split on the floor like a broken jaw. Smoke thinned, tugged by a foul wind. Men moved in twos, torches high, dogs at heel. They didn't rush. The work was done.

Jed slid flat behind a toppled shelf and watched. Torchlight cut faces into edges. One bare-armed, freckles across muscle. Another bald, scalp inked with curling script. A third with teeth filed sharp, grin too practiced. Different men, moving the same—loose, efficient—the walk of killers finishing.

"Shiny ones," one said, cutting a necklace from a woman's throat. "Pot's still warm," another muttered, kicking broth over stone. "Check stragglers," a third said, prodding until the body stayed still. "Captain doesn't like waste."

The wolf-hide captain stepped into view. The men straightened without meaning to. Dogs went still. His pale eyes scanned the broken stone. His jaw looked carved for orders. He lifted his torch, studied the claw marks gouged into the wall, then drove the brand head-down into the rubble to choke the last of the smoke.

"Captain," someone called from the far spur. "North run's clear." "Check the alcoves," another answered. "Veynar wants it clean."

Veynar wiped his palm on the pelt, adjusted the sword-belt at his hip, and turned away. He stepped over a child's shoe and never looked down.

Chapter 3

What Stayed

When they left, they left quiet. Jed waited longer than quiet. He waited until the smoke drifted again and the heat pulled its teeth back. Only then did he roll onto his hands and knees. His limbs shook under him, not from weakness but with bones hollowed, rattling inside him. He crawled to where the sleeping shelf had been.

Yarra lay beneath the roof-stones, as if the earth had decided the world was too loud and put her to bed. Her eyes were open. The old net sling was shredded under her belly, where she had wrapped it tight around Kep and tried to make a tunnel with her body. Her hands were still curved, the way they cupped small heads, held water, held firelight.

Jed's throat closed, a muscle locking against itself. His fingers trembled as he pushed her lids down, grit catching on his skin. He had done the same for his father once, after a cave-in that had been no one's fault. Then, his hands had been steady. Now, he had to press until his nails bit his own skin. He had not known a body could carry the weight of the whole world. Now he knew.

He dug for Kep until his nails tore and the tips of his fingers wept blood. His breath came ragged, not from effort but from the panic that he might never find him. When he did, the boy was small. Jed knew where all the bones should be, and they were there, and it did not matter.

There was a way to lift a child when you were afraid you would break him. Jed did not use it. His hands shook so hard that gentleness would have turned to dropping. He had nothing gentle left. He gathered what he could into the net and tied it with the ease of a knot that had served him all his life, though his hands cramped on the rope until he had to bite down on the cord to steady them.

He took Yarra's wrist and untied the red thread she had worn there long enough to blanch the skin beneath. His fingers fumbled the knot twice before it came free. He bound it around his own wrist and pulled it tight until it bit. He found her knife under a plank and slid it into his belt. He took Kep's pebble-puzzle and shoved it into his mouth because his hands were busy and he could not let go of anything else.

He carried them together to the mark-stone. His legs threatened to fold at every step, but his jaw clenched so tight it kept him upright. He set them down on a shelf that had not fallen and carved a line into the broken face with Yarra's knife. The steel skittered. His arm cramped. The crack ran down through other people's signs, through his own, through the neat little square he had cut for Kep two moons ago. He cut anyway. He kept cutting until the knife was warm and his wrist ached and his knuckles split. The new mark said nothing and everything at once.

He did not send them to sea. The tide had fed his people. He was not going to give it this. He stacked stone on stone until his back tried to leave him. His hands split and bled on the rock. He made the pile too high and it fell and he made it again. When he could not lift another rock he leaned his forehead against the heap and breathed stone and salt and blood until his chest seized in sobs that had no sound.

He wanted to scream. He had a very clear picture of how to do it—throw his head back and let the sound tear his throat, spit blood in the dark, break on it like surf. His mouth opened, but the scream broke into a smaller sound instead, a hiccuped gasp that shamed him. It was worse.

His hands kept moving. They found others, because that's what hands do when the heart refuses to stop. He found the chief under a beam and pulled him free, muscles shaking. He found a hatchling not his and wrapped it in a piece of

Yarra's old shawl, hands clumsy, jaw grinding. He found the shiver of a breath under a pile of nets and dragged out Tesh from the fish-curers, her ribs clicking like sticks. She lived long enough to say, "The dogs," in a voice that did not sound like a person.

Jed's hands twitched around hers until her pulse stopped. Then he sat with her until her body cooled, staring at nothing. His vision tunneled. His lips moved with no sound. When he finally stood, he swayed, bracing himself against the stone with a palm that left blood behind.

He broke open a dry storage niche with a pry bar and found skins of water that had not turned sweet and sacks of salt. He took a coil of rope. He took a hammer. He took three iron nails. He took a little bag of coins no one had needed because money did not matter under rock. His fingers closed over each with mechanical force, movements jerking like someone half-asleep.

He looked again at the pile he had made for Yarra and Kep. The crack down the mark-stone looked like a mouth. His vision blurred until the crack itself seemed to grin at him.

He said their names one last time, his voice raw and shredded, not because he meant to leave them but because the names needed saying while they were still names. Then he turned toward the shaft.

The way out hurt. Smoke does not stop because you ask it to. His throat burned raw by the time he found air cold enough to blister his lungs. His eyes poured water until he could barely see. He crawled the last stretch on hands that dragged like stone and came into night like a fish gulping beyond the net.

He had always hated the sky. This one hated him back. It was too big. It had too many stars. It pretended not to see the smoke rising slow and patient from the hidden mouths under rock.

The world above had the noises of the world above: gulls muttering in their sleep, distant water hissing at stone, a cart wheel complaining somewhere far off. Jed turned his head toward Grayhaven instinctively, because hate and need have the same compass. The city squatted on the coast like a patient wound. Its lights were small, a line of teeth against black water. Someone laughed out there. Someone sang, off-key and slow, the way only people who have eaten sing.

Jed's knees wanted to fold. He wanted to crawl back into the hole and lie down with his dead and stop. Instead he stood, fists tight enough that his nails bit into his palms. He picked a direction away from anything that might ask him for words, and walked. His legs worked. It felt like treachery.

He found a thicket above the tide line where the wind had bullied the brush flat. He did not think he had slept, but he woke. He woke to hunger big enough to eat him and thirst bigger. His belly cramped. His head throbbed. He found his way to a seep in a crease of rock and drank by cupping his hands until the water tasted like iron. He ate dried fish from the storage sacks because the body demands before it asks permission.

The second night he made a little fire with driftwood and hated himself for liking the heat. He sat with the rope in his lap and the hammer by his knee and Yarra's knife in his hand. His fingers flexed and cramped around the hilt. He did not clean it. The salt did it for him.

He told himself he would go back to the pile of stones at dawn and make it better. He told himself he would carry the hatchlings to the sea, because that is what you do. He told himself he would take Hesk's old bones and find a tide pool deep enough to hold a raft.

At dawn, his body refused him. His knees buckled when he tried to turn back. Not because the work did not need doing. Because something else had taken his legs and refused.

He cut a strip from his shirt with shaking hands and tied Yarra's knife to the inside of his forearm. He tied Kep's red thread tighter, until his hand tingled. He took the three iron nails and put them in his pocket. He did not know why—only that hands with nothing to hold will do damage to themselves.

By the third day, the smoke from the warrens was thin enough to pretend it was a cloud. People in Grayhaven stood on the quay and watched anyway. Jed watched them from a dune, chest aching with each breath, and tried to understand the mechanics of a laugh this close to the smell he could not get out of his nose.

When a dockhand finally wandered up the beach to piss and spotted him in the brush, the man started, then relaxed when he saw what he was. "Vermin," the man said, giving a lazy kick with his boot to see if Jed would flinch.

12

Jed did not move. The part of him that might have cared had already been buried under stone.

The man grinned. "You lot breed like fish. Don't worry. Plenty of holes to crawl into."

Jed's eyes dropped to the man's boot—good leather, badly stitched, the heel peg loose. He should have felt anger. Instead, he only noted the flaw, the way a corpse notes a draft.

He lifted his gaze back to the city. His voice came out flat, dug from stone. "Is there coin for dead rats in your city?"

The dockhand barked a laugh. "Bring me tails and I'll give you buttons."

Jed's jaw twitched. "Buttons fall off. Coin buys bread."

"Bread goes moldy," the man shot back, smirking.

Jed said nothing. His silence was heavier than words, the silence of someone already standing in his own grave. The dockhand squinted, then lost interest the way people do when you're smaller than their time. He turned back toward Grayhaven, heel peg ticking against stone as he went.

Jed watched him go and did not follow. His hands ached from clenching. There was nothing to follow. Only forward.

He walked the beach until he found the skiff. It had been thrown up by a storm or a bad captain. Its ribs stuck out like a fish left to bleach. The planks were warped, the stern split, the keel scarred where it had fought rock and lost. Jed crouched in its shadow and laid his hand on its side. The wood was warm. He hit it once with his fist, not hard. The sound it made was hollow and honest.

He looked back toward the smoke. Then forward toward the city. He curled under the skiff and slept. In the morning, it would still be there, waiting.

Chapter 4

What Moved Forward

He became something smaller: a creature that did not die.

At low tide, he crawled across the black rocks, knees scraping raw, fingers prying at seams of barnacle and shell. The mussels clung hard to the stone, harder than his bleeding hands. He worked them loose with Yarra's knife until his knuckles split and salt stung the cuts. Each one he dropped into the pail thudded like something that should beat, but didn't. Gulls wheeled and shrieked above. He hissed back, low, until his throat ached.

The pail wasn't much. Brine sloshed around half a dozen shells, most chipped or thin. But it was something. Something he could carry forward, even if nothing else had followed him out of the smoke.

By dusk, he hunched into Grayhaven, shoulders low, walking like a shadow that had forgotten its shape. The market stalls spat light and noise into the salt wind. Fishwives shouted prices. Men argued over ropes and salt-pork. Jed kept his head down, ears flat, eyes quick for the edges no one else cared about.

He found a rough plank table stacked with day-old loaves, crusts going hard. Behind it stood a woman—arms thick as rope, apron dusted with flour, eyes sharp as a fishhook. Her hair was pinned back in a severe bun that hadn't shifted through a whole day's heat, and her frame carried the kind of heavy strength carved for barrels and ovens rather than finery. She was snapping at a boy who'd tried to take bread without coin.

15

Jed set the pail down. The mussels rattled.

Her eyes flicked to him, quick and cutting. "What's this, then? Rat got himself a bucket?"

He said nothing. Just nudged the pail forward.

She bent, plucked one out, turned it in her hand. The shell flaked salt onto her palm. "Ugly things. Look like they crawled out of a drunk man's beard. You trying to poison me, kobold?"

Jed kept his gaze on the bread. His stomach twisted so hard it felt like it might crawl out of him too.

Her laugh cracked out sudden, rough. "Saints, you're no fun at all. Don't even twitch when a woman insults your catch. What are you, stone?"

He didn't answer.

She tossed the mussel back into the pail. "Eh. Bread for these'll only keep a gull alive. But—" She tore the heel off a loaf, shoved it across the plank. "—gulls eat, don't they? Mara, if you're asking. Not that you did."

Jed reached, slow, like the air around them might snap.

"Careful," Mara said. "Wouldn't want the rat to bite." But her eyes softened a notch, like a knot loosening in the rope.

He took the bread. Didn't thank her. Couldn't. But the corner of his mouth almost remembered how to move.

Jed sat on the dock with his knees drawn up, the stale bread in his hands. He tore it slow, chewing though it scraped his gums. Hard bread, yes. But made by care, and care was rarer than coin.

"Storms take the best of us."

The voice came from his right. Jed turned, wary.

A man sat on a coil of rope, broad through the shoulders, a sailor's gut settled under his belt. A bald scalp gleamed faintly in the lamplight; a dark beard, shot with gray, edged his jaw. He looked out at the sea instead of at Jed, a flask hanging loose in his hand.

"Don't sit like that," the man went on. "You'll get barnacles."

Jed said nothing. He pinched the crust tighter.

The man finally looked at him, one eye narrowed as if measuring whether to throw him back into the tide. He tipped the flask toward Jed. "They used to call me Brann, back when I still sailed for coin. Now I just sit here and pretend the sea remembers me. Ale?"

Jed hesitated.

"Take it," Brann said. "Even rats know how to swim when the ship's sinking. And you look like you're letting yourself drown."

Jed took the flask, drank. The ale burned down raw, and he nearly spat it back up.

Brann's laugh broke across the dock, full-bellied, startling a gull into flight. "That's better. Sound of a man with lungs. Better than gnawing sorrow alone."

Jed wiped his mouth with the back of his hand. The bread sat heavy in his lap. "I wasn't drowning," he muttered.

Brann leaned in, grin wide with broken teeth. "Then what are you, eh? Sitting here with eyes like a grave? The sea doesn't pity. It takes. Men take, too. You either spit back or you vanish. I've seen both."

The words struck like stones. Men take. Jed remembered the voices in the smoke, the mercenaries laughing as the warrens burned. He remembered the name they'd spoken like it belonged to them—Veynar. He had not seen the man. Only heard him named. But it was enough.

He gave the flask back. His hand didn't shake.

Brann studied him a moment, then gave a short nod, as though satisfied. "Good. You'll live yet." He swigged from the flask and leaned back, humming an old tune into the wind.

Jed sat with the stale bread in his lap, staring into the tide, and felt the seed take root. He could not bring Yarra or Kep back. But maybe he could make Veynar pay.

He went back to the skiff and lay down with the knife under his arm and the nails in his pocket. He listened to the water breathe. His throat ached and would not stop. He did not sleep so much as pass into a place that was not awake and was not safe.

In the gray before dawn, he opened his eyes and told himself a simple thing: men had come because someone had paid them. They would be paid again—unless someone made it cost more than it paid.

He was small. He was poor. He did not own a spear that would not splinter on a shield. He owned a sling that threw stones and a knife that cut things he loved and things he did not. He owned an awl with a cracked handle he had glued three times. He carried nails in his pocket. Tools, all of them—and he was learning they had more than one use.

He stood. He walked to the line where wet sand turned dry and drew the mark again with his heel. The tide hissed at him. He hissed back.

Grayhaven woke by degrees: gulls first, curses second, the creak of rope and timber last. It sounded almost peaceful. Jed knew better.

He watched long enough to see the day take hold, then turned his back on it—not to walk away, but to walk the beach until he found a place where the rocks made a low wall and the wind made a high noise. He liked to pretend the wind spoke. Today it was mute. He said the names again into that nothing—Yarra, Kep—and when the sound disappeared, he pretended that meant they had heard him.

That night, he meant to go to the city. Not to shout, not to weep. To look. To see how men moved when they were not breaking things. To learn where they forgot to look because they believed nothing important could be small.

He tied the knife tight and tested the sling twice. He filled his pocket with three smooth stones. He moved the nails to the other pocket—change for a trade no one else would see.

The day ground across him like a slow wheel. When the light fell, he rose. He walked toward Grayhaven with the sea at his shoulder and the smell of smoke, old and new, in his lungs. He did not think of what he was not. He thought of the mark he would cut on stone where the tide could not have it.

He would not become a story yet. Stories were for other people's mouths. He would become something else first: a shape in the corner of an eye, a footfall that is not a footfall, a hand that knows where leather gives.

The watchman on the outer quay yawned as Jed passed under the arch. "Curfew's for rats," he said without looking down.

Jed lowered his head and kept walking.

Somewhere inside the city, a man in a wolf-hide drank someone else's wine and licked smoke off his teeth without tasting it. Jed could imagine the smile, a hinge turning toward him.

He lifted his face once to the wind and tasted salt, tar, and the iron tang that never left. He let that be the last gentle thing he did that night.

He walked into Grayhaven. The mark was already waiting in his palm.

Chapter 5

Marks in the Stone

He walked into Grayhaven. The mark was already waiting in his palm.

Streets folded tight around him, stone sweating brine and smoke. Torches guttered in iron throats and turned the alleys into teeth—light, dark, light, dark—like a mouth about to close. Meat-fat burned somewhere ahead, piss steamed where a drunk had slid down a wall, and the tide rasped at the quay as if filing the city down to a blade.

Jed kept small. Tail wrapped tight, shoulders rounded, claws tucked in his sleeves. Men did not look behind themselves here. They laughed with their throats open and their knife-hilts loose and thought danger lived in stories told by other mouths. He counted their blind spots the way he once counted stitches—thumb, forefinger, pull.

The alley where it happened stank of fish guts tipped from a bucket. Scales glued to the stones like old coins. A cat watched from a window slit with the bored eyes of something that knew how nights ended.

The boy was already cornered.

Dead end: three strides wide, eight deep. One exit behind the men. The boy—no more than ten—had his spine to the far wall, crust clutched tight, ribs like tally marks under gray skin.

Three dock-thick men ringed him in a loose half circle at two paces. Left: crooked nose, empty hands. Center: a cloak patched from sailcloth squares, a

21

knife low at his belt. Right: a cudgel, wrist wrapped in old rope. Rotgut on their breath. Boots hard enough to break a small chest.

"Look at it clutch," crooked-nose said, grinning through black nubs of teeth. "King of scraps."

The boy tucked the bread closer.

The cloaked one prodded him with two fingers as if counting bones. "One—two—three—saints, I can play this all night." He shoved. The back of the boy's head knocked stone and emptied his breath.

"Quit playing," the cudgel man spat. "I'm hungry."

Jed pressed himself to the left wall. Slime cold under his palm. Knife sheathed. Sling already looped to his wrist. He told himself he'd come here to watch, to learn the city. Not to bleed.

"Please," the boy breathed, so soft the word never left his lips.

Laughter like torches flaring. Hands reached. A boot pinned the wrist that held the bread. The crust fell face-down into the muck.

Jed saw Kep instead—eyes wide as night when the smoke pulled him sideways out of the world. The hinge inside him turned.

His hand was already on a stone.

The sling purred once. The first shot clipped the cloaked man's ear—meat and blood, not temple. He yelped and turned his head away from the boy.

Second stone hissed past crooked-nose and cracked the wall a hand's breadth from his cheek. Both men flinched toward the sound.

Jed dropped the sling, drew the knife, and went low.

Cloak lunged. Jed slipped inside the grab, raked calf with four quick claws, and skipped back. Weight went to the cut leg; the man stumbled.

Cudgel swung high for Jed's head. Jed ducked; the end still glanced his shoulder. Pain flashed. He let it pull him sideways and rolled with it, coming up against the left-hand wall—shoulder braced, knife forward.

Crooked-nose rushed. Jed planted, tail snaked behind the man's ankles, and he yanked. Crooked-nose pitched forward. Jed met him coming down—short, up under the ribs. Weight went slack.

Cudgel came again, horizontal. Jed raised his forearm, took the blow on scale—bad trade, but it saved his skull. He stepped inside the arc and cut the inner thigh. The man's leg buckled. Jed looped the dropped sling across his throat from behind and hauled. The cudgel thudded once against stone, then twice softer. Breath rattled, then stopped.

The cloaked man had his knife out now, blood on his ear and rage on his face. "You rat—"

Jed didn't answer. He feinted high; the blade chased the lie. Jed's knife slid low, below the navel. Twist. The man folded around the hurt and slid down the wall.

Silence rushed in. Only the boy's breath left.

Jed stayed low, lungs grinding, ribs hot with fire. Crooked-nose gargled wetly on the stones. Jed moved because silence mattered more than mercy. The knife opened throats—quick, clean—not for pride. For quiet.

He wiped the blade on cloak-scraps. The boy was already gone, bare feet pattering away into another mouth of dark, bread clutched tight.

Jed hated how his claws shook as they untied cloaks. He hated the guilty clink of coins in his palm. He hated how badly he wanted boots that would keep glass out of his feet. He took them anyway. He took the sword a man had never drawn. He wound the pouch-string tight around his wrist, because dropping it would have felt like surrender.

There was a clean patch of wall where the slime hadn't reached. He set the blade there. Slow lines. Crooked. A child's drawing of a memory. His clan's mark stood pale against black stone.

He touched his forehead to it. The grit dug his skin raw. Salt or iron touched his lips; he couldn't tell which. The alley gave no answer. He had learned not to ask.

The city roared elsewhere—drums, bells, a woman's voice in laughter. No one turned in here. Not tonight.

He dragged the sword with him, its tip scratching a line the tide began eating as soon as he made it. His hands cramped into claws that wouldn't unclench. When the wrecked skiff loomed out of the dark, ribs up like a carcass, he nearly wept for the mercy of wood that didn't move.

He worked until work steadied him. Twine looped into snares. A trip-line low across driftwood stakes. A pot of stones ready to fall loud as a bell. He cut the toes from the boots and stitched the leather back with net-thread. He sealed seams of the skiff with pitch scraped from its belly. He leaned the sword where he could reach it, even knowing it wasn't his friend.

When he finally lay down, knife tucked under his arm, the wreck didn't feel like a grave. It felt like a room with a barred door.

Dawn bruised pale above the water. The tide had licked his sword-line flat. Bells tolled from Grayhaven. He touched the cracked gunwale. He touched the knife, still sticky under the handle. He let his lip lift without showing teeth.

Men had paid to turn his home into smoke. Men had smiled while it happened. They would pay again, unless someone taught them to stop smiling.

He would learn their alleys. He would learn when the Watch turned heads and where dogs refused to go. He would map the city in chalk on his palm until the lines made a net. He would not roar. He would not be a story. He would be the hand in the dark, the stone that struck first.

He tied the sling's knot tight. He weighed three smooth stones. He checked the trip-line with his heel and let the pot of stones clack once to hear its promise. He walked with soft-soled boots that said nothing on sand.

The wreck held behind him. Grayhaven waited in front, all knives and gulls. The mark in his palm felt heavier than the coins at his wrist. The base was made. The hunt would begin.

Chapter 6

Chapter Six — The Docks Wake

Morning came with gulls screaming and the docks already heaving like a ship's deck in storm. Men shouted rope commands as a brigantine slid into berth, its hull scraping barnacles against stone. Nets hit the planks with wet thuds, spilling silver fish that slapped and writhed until boys scooped them into baskets. A hammer beat rhythm on a hull; a saw sang as it bit through pine; a barrel rolled loose and a dockhand cursed as it clipped his shin.

Jed wove through the chaos with shoulders hunched and tail tight to his leg, a shadow trying not to be noticed among bigger shadows. The stink of tar and fish guts clung in his nose. He slipped past a woman shaking scales from her apron, ducked a coil of rope tossed without looking, sidestepped the splash of bilge water dumped from a pail.

The bread smell cut through it all—warm, coarse, sharp with yeast. He followed it as though it had a string tied to his chest.

Mara's stall stood braced against the wind, nets flapping above it like banners, though what she sold was bread. Loaves stacked high, crusts browned hard, crumbs dusting her plank. She was in full roar, apron smeared dark, a basket of crusts at her hip.

"I said two loaves, not one and a half, you stingy bastard! Think I don't know my own weight of flour?" She snatched the short measure from a fishmonger's boy and cuffed his ear. He yelped and bolted, dropping the loaf.

Jed stopped at the edge of the crowd, clutching the copper in his pocket. His claws worried the coin's worn edge until he forced his hand out. He placed it on her plank.

Mara's eyes, dark and hooked as an anchor, flicked to him. "Back again? Careful, ratling—keep turning up and folk'll think you belong."

He said nothing. Just kept his head low.

"Bread for a copper, then." She shoved a heel across. Her voice was brusque, but her hand lingered on the loaf a fraction too long—as though testing if he might snatch it like a thief. When he didn't, she let go.

Jed curled his claws around it. The smell near undid him.

"Morning to you, Mara!"

The voice boomed like surf. Brann came ambling out of the press, shoulders broad enough to part sailors. He carried a string of dried fish and the grin of a man who'd already had his first swig.

"Already yelling before noon, I see." He leaned an elbow on the stall. "Makes a man feel young again."

"You're late paying your tab," Mara snapped.

"And yet here I stand, coin in hand," Brann said cheerfully, tossing a copper down. "Two crusts, and don't pretend they're fresh."

She smirked despite herself and turned to fetch them.

Brann's gaze landed on Jed. "Ah, the quiet one. Morning. You find sleep enough, or does the tide keep you whispering?"

Jed hesitated. Then, rough with disuse: "I slept."

Brann's brows rose. "He speaks! Thought maybe you'd taken a vow." He tore a hunk of crust and chewed, talking around it. "You got a name, boy?"

Jed's throat worked. "Jed."

"Jed." Brann nodded. "Good name. Short. Sticks." His grin widened, though his eyes were softer. "And what's a Jed doing in Grayhaven, eh? Place like this swallows folk whole."

26

Jed stared at the loaf in his hand. The words came like pulling teeth. "Lost things. Family. Clan. Thought maybe... start over."

The crowd pressed loud around them—hawkers calling "Fresh cod! Six for a copper!", a sailor cursing as a crate cracked and spilled nails, gulls shrieking overhead—but Mara stilled at that. Her arms crossed, flour dust rising from her apron. Brann's grin faded at the edges.

"Saints above," Mara muttered. "Poor scrap."

Brann tilted his head, beard hiding the downturn of his mouth. Then he clapped Jed's shoulder, sudden and solid. "Then here's to starting over. Dock's good for that. Sea washes more sins clean than priests do."

Jed flinched at the touch, but didn't pull away.

Mara's tone sharpened again, like she couldn't let pity linger. "If you're hanging about, I can put you to use. Crates don't move themselves, and I've no patience for lazy boys sniffing after free bread. You work mornings—sweep, carry, fetch what I point at. Pay's bread and a copper each week. But if you so much as think of stealing—"

Jed's eyes lifted, flat and steady. "I won't."

She held his gaze a beat, then snorted. "We'll see."

Brann chuckled. "There, you've gone and got yourself a trade. Better than rotting in alleys."

Jed tucked the bread close, the copper gone from his pocket, but another coin dropped into his mind—the name Veynar, turning heavy as lead. He let the noise of the docks mask his next words.

"What kind of men?"

Brann squinted at him, then shrugged. "All kinds. Merchants fat with coin. Guildsmen mean as wolves about their cut. Sellswords, too—plenty of them since the war down south. Mercenary bands drift in, drift out. Drink half the taverns dry, leave with pockets heavier or heads lighter."

Jed's claws pressed the crust. "Mercenaries?"

"Aye." Brann's grin turned crooked. "You'll know 'em when you see 'em. Wolf hides, crow feathers, iron badges—every crew struts with some mark. They want you to know what steel they sell."

Jed dropped his gaze quickly, as though it were idle curiosity. "And the city? Streets twist."

Mara snorted. "Of course they twist. Grayhaven wasn't built, it grew. Like barnacles on a hull. Market's the heart, everything else spirals out. You'll learn, if you've eyes."

"I have eyes," Jed murmured.

"Then use them," Mara shot back, but her mouth softened just a fraction. She pushed a crate toward him with her boot. "Start with that one. Fish guts to the pier-end. Let's see if you're worth the copper."

Jed spent the morning bent under crates, the wood biting his shoulders, fish blood running cold down his arms. He swept the stone where scales clung in heaps, shoved refuse to the tide, hauled ropes until his claws split. No one thanked him. Few looked twice.

But he listened.

Dockhands muttered of "three blades found cut up in the gutter" and "some devil stalking the alleys." Sailors swapped versions like cards—a shadow-dog, a knife-witch, even a ghost of the drowned. No one said kobold. No one said rat.

Jed kept his head low, shoulders rounded, eyes on the work. His tail wrapped tight so it wouldn't flick when he heard the word mercenaries.

By midday, the sun cut through the haze. A band of sellswords swaggered along the quay, their boots louder than the gulls. One wore a wolf-hide, another crow feathers braided into his beard. Steel clinked at their sides. They laughed too loud, shoved boys aside without looking.

Jed froze, broom in hand.

The wolf-hide man was broad, not the one from the warrens—but close enough in stance to burn the name Veynar across Jed's vision. His chest rose shallow, ears ringing with remembered barks. Smoke seemed to crawl down the back of his throat again, tar-thick and choking. He saw Kep's eyes wide and shining just before the roof came down. He heard Yarra's steady voice—Back—and the sound of stone breaking.

His claws dug grooves into the broom handle until splinters bit. His tail coiled tight as a knot around his leg, the tip twitching like it wanted to strike. His breath hitched and broke shallow.

The sellswords passed within arm's reach. One reeked of sweat and pitch, another of sour ale, another dragged a scarred sword across the planks just to hear the scrape. They never looked down. Their laughter gusted over him, rough as the smoke that had pulled his world to pieces.

Only when the tavern door closed behind them did Jed breathe again. The broom shook in his grip. He bent quickly to sweep fish scales so no one would see his hands tremble.

That night he dragged his body back to the wrecked skiff. Salt stung his cracked hands as he washed them in the tide, scrubbed every trace of fish and blood away. He laid the bread aside, untouched, and sat staring at the black water.

Three men dead. His claws had done it. His teeth, his knife, his tail.

He waited for shame. It came, but it was thin beside the coil tightening in his chest. He remembered the boy running free with bread, and the mercenary's laugh in the smoke.

Hunter, not prey.

The skiff creaked as the tide shifted. Jed looked at its broken ribs, the patchwork pitch, the driftwood posts he had sunk around it like teeth. Not home. A lair. A base.

He tore into the bread at last, chewing slow, eyes fixed on the city lights.

He would have to be careful. Never let them see him coming. Never let them suspect.

And one day, he would find Veynar Blackfang.

Chapter 7

The First Hunt

Jed sat in his den beneath the upturned hull, salt-soaked boards curving above like the ribs of a carcass. The broken skiff leaked when it rained and stank of tar, but it was shelter. He sat cross-legged on the black fur cloak he'd claimed from his first kill, Yarra's knife across his knees. He drew it against a whetstone—slow, steady.

Every scrape carried memory: ribs bruised from fists, blood slick on cobbles, the clumsy thrash of the alley fight. If it had been Veynar, he thought, I'd be ash in the tide by now.

He flexed his claws against the fur, let his tail coil tight. He breathed. Learn. Be quieter. Be sharper.

The sling lay beside him, stones chosen smooth and round. He was not strong, but he could be quick. Small. Unseen.

When the moon lifted over the masts, Jed rose.

Grayhaven at night was a different beast. Lanterns swung above the streets, casting broken pools of light and long seams of dark. Dice clattered in doorways. Men pissed against walls. The Watch trudged in pairs, pikes drooping, lanterns yawning arcs through smoke.

Jed moved in silence through gutters and shadows. His kind had always known how to disappear in the seams of things. Tonight, though, he was not just hiding. He was hunting.

Not the strong ones. Not yet, he told himself. Find the hunters of smaller prey.

Laughter found him first. A woman's strained protest.

The cut ran between tavern and warehouse: three strides wide, ten deep, open to the street on Jed's side, choked by stacked kegs at the far end. One lantern burned back on the street behind him; moonlight caught on wet stone. The woman had her back to the kegs, body curved around a boy who clung to her skirts, sobbing.

Two thugs blocked the way out—shoulders wide, breath sour with ale. Left: knife hung loose by his thigh. Right: cudgel low, wrist wrapped in old rope.

"Out late, eh?" Cudgel sneered. "Basket looks heavy. Let us take it. Might keep the lad too—he looks quick."

The woman jerked her arm free. The boy cried louder.

Jed's breath caught. Smoke. Yarra clutching Kep. Empty arms. Silence after.

Loadout, then: sling looped on his left wrist; Yarra's knife sheathed at his right hip. Wall at his spine. Four paces to Knife, five to Cudgel, two to the woman.

He palmed a stone. Drew once, twice—and loosed past Knife's ear.

The rock cracked loud against the right-hand wall. Both heads snapped toward the sound.

Jed was already moving.

He slid along the left wall, darted low past Cudgel's outside shoulder, and raked four claws across the man's calf.

A roar. A blind boot came back hard.

Crack.

Pain lit Jed's ribs white. Air fled his chest.

He let the kick spin him, rolled with it—tail whipping stone—and came up crouched between the thugs and the woman, knife out to keep space.

Cudgel swung horizontal at Jed's head.

Thud.

Too slow ducking—the end kissed his jaw and ear. Stars burst. He slammed shoulder-first into the wall and felt the world tilt.

Knife seized Jed's scruff and hauled him up like vermin. Jed twisted, jaws snapping. Teeth found wrist. Hot copper filled his mouth. Knife screamed and smashed him down.

Get up. Get up.

Jed cut blind as he surged, blade angling high. The point slid into the warm hollow of the armpit. Blood spilled hot over his hand. Knife's grip faltered; Jed dropped to his knees, boots scrabbling on slick stone.

Cudgel limped in, rage carved deep. He threw his left. Jed ducked the first, took the second across the jaw—white again, fresh stars.

He answered with his tail—snaked it round Cudgel's ankle, yanked. The big man staggered. Jed leapt up his back like a mast, sling cord snapping across the throat. He braced both feet against the man's hips and hauled.

Cudgel clawed at the cord, stumbling backward. He slammed Jed against the wall—once, twice. Jed held on, teeth bared, knife punching under the collarbone once. Twice. The man toppled. Jed rode him down, tightening until the rattle quit and the weight went slack.

Knife lurched forward, free wrist dripping, cudgel forgotten, rage trying to make up for blood lost. He raised the empty hand as if it held steel.

Jed rolled off the corpse. The cudgel smashed stone where his skull had been; shards spat across his muzzle. Jed slashed low, claws tearing shin. Knife stumbled.

Jed drove in close and up—blade under the jaw, through the soft hollow. A convulsion. A cough of red. Then stillness.

Silence fell, save for the boy's sobs and Jed's rasping breath.

He crouched small, blood slick on claws and teeth, and forced the knife down. "You're safe now," he said, rough but soft. "No one will touch you."

The woman trembled but did not flee. Jed lifted the basket, set it carefully at her feet, then let a single claw brush the boy's hair—gentle as a memory. In Draconic, he whispered what he had once whispered to Kep: Safe now, little one. Safe.

She nodded, eyes wet, and hurried away, clutching her son.

Lantern light flared at the alley's mouth. Boots on stone. Watch.

Jed dragged one body behind a barrel, shoved the other into the deeper shadow beside the kegs, and dove into a midden heap. Rot closed over him.

Lantern glow swept close. Boots splashed.

"Smells like the dockers've been dumping guts again," one muttered.

"Leave it. Come dawn, it's the fishwives' problem."

They passed. The light thinned.

Jed waited until the quiet settled again. His claws unclenched from muck, shaking. He crawled out, scraped skin raw against brick, and dunked himself in a rain barrel until the water ran pink.

Back in his den under the skiff, he stripped, doused himself in seawater, and collapsed on the fur cloak. Knife under his arm, he stared at the hull's shadowed ribs.

He whispered Yarra's name. Kep's.

He hated himself. And yet—beneath the shame, steady as tide—came another thought:

This is practice. This is how a hunter learns.

He closed his eyes. Not to dream. To plan.

Chapter 8

Chapter Eight — Whispers on the Docks

J ed woke before dawn, breath fogging against the ribs of the broken hull
that sheltered him. The wrecked skiff had long since lost its keel, its belly
split and propped against pilings to make a crooked roof. Beneath it, he had
carved out a space barely wide enough for his body and a heap of old nets.
The black fur cloak—taken from the man he'd killed on his first night—lay
beneath him as bedding. It smelled of smoke and blood even after endless
rinses, but it was soft. In the dark, the nap caught against his cheek the way
hair once had. He pressed his snout into it for a heartbeat, then pushed
himself up.

The tide had left the boards slick. Jed's tail dragged through the damp as
he crawled out, blinking into the salt-stained dawn. The harbor was already
alive: gulls bickered over a fish spine, sailors shouted while hauling lines taut,
and the sharp tang of tar mixed with the sweet rot of seaweed left to dry.
A fishmonger banged a cleaver against his block in time with the ship bells
ringing out the change of watch.

Mara's shop stood crooked in the line of dockside stalls, walls patched with
driftwood and shutters painted once-red, now peeled to gray. A canvas windbreak
snapped above the doorway. Racks of cooling loaves filled the front, steam lifting

in faint ghosts. Bread peels, ladles, and long bread knives hung in neat rows behind the counter, edges catching the thin light.

Jed lingered in the doorway.

"If you're here to work," Mara snapped without looking up from weighing out flour, "then work. Don't stand there like a gull waiting for scraps."

Her voice was smoke-thick, steady as an anchor chain. Jed lowered his head, lifted the nearest sack, and staggered under its weight to the corner where she pointed. His arms burned before he set it down, but the work steadied him. He stacked flour, split kindling, swept flour dust from the floor until it filled the grooves in his claws, scraped baked-on crust from pans until his shoulders ached.

Mara watched him with hawk eyes, arms folded over her apron. Every time he slowed, she barked a new order: "Faster." "Not there, against the wall." "If you drop that, lizard, I'll dock your pay before I've given it."

The hours turned with the tide. The bell over the door clanged again and again as customers shuffled in—dockwives wrapped in patched shawls, children tugging at skirts, fishers with split knuckles and sea-worn boots. They traded coins and gossip in equal measure.

"You hear about Southshore?" one woman said, laying down a purse of coppers. "Two men gutted like fish."

"Aye," her companion replied, voice hushed as though the shadows listened. "Said it weren't no man. Some rat-beast. Eyes like lanterns."

Jed's claws tightened on the broom handle. He bent lower, sweeping slower, listening.

A sailor spat into a bucket. "You lot believe every fireside tale. Men killed men, same as ever. Too much drink, too many knives."

"Then why'd the Watch say they found claw marks?" the woman whispered. "Rat-dragon, they're calling it. Big as a hound, they say. Teeth like sickles."

The name twisted in Jed's gut. He swept harder until wood rasped under the straw. Mara set the woman's loaves on the counter with a thump and said, "Monsters don't haunt Grayhaven. Men do. Folk see shadows and want a story. Stories don't keep ovens fed."

36

Her voice was firm, dismissive—but when Jed risked a glance, her eyes cut to him for a heartbeat. A quick weight. Then gone.

By midday, Mara shoved a heel of bread into his hand. "Eat outside. You're dripping sweat into my trays."

Jed slipped out into the dockside air. He sat on the planks, gnawing the hard crust while gulls wheeled above. The water slapped against the quay, carrying the stink of bilge and salt.

"First day's the worst," Brann's voice called, bright over the noise. The man dropped beside him, the grin on his scarred face tilted as if he carried jokes and ghosts in equal measure. He pulled a loaf from his coat, tore it, and shoved half into Jed's hands without asking.

"Mara works you like a dog?"

Jed chewed slow. "Or sees cheap labor."

Brann barked a laugh, slapping his knee. "Both, then. She's as soft as a barnacle, but if she keeps you fed, count yourself lucky." He leaned back on his elbows, watching the gulls. For a moment the grin thinned. "Strange talk today. Southshore—two men carved up. Some say a beast. Some say worse. The Watch is on edge. Not often Grayhaven whispers about monsters."

Jed's tail curled close around his leg. "Monsters live in men," he said softly. "Not alleys."

Brann studied him—warm eyes, heavy with things seen. Then he grinned again, clapping Jed's shoulder. "True enough. Still—keep your head down. Watch has long spears and shorter patience."

Jed nodded, quiet. He let Brann talk, and asked small questions that sounded like curiosity about markets and taverns, about work. Brann, good-natured as ever, told him. Lantern routes and blind corners sifted themselves into Jed's ears, a net of streets he could move through without catching.

The afternoon wore on. Jed hauled more sacks, stacked wood, cleaned peels until they shone, scrubbed soot from the oven's mouth. By the time the sun slid toward the water, the shop grew quiet. Mara was counting coin, lips tight in the rhythm of numbers, when the bell over the door rang.

37

Boots struck wood—not hurried, not humble. Heavy. Confident. Sweat and leather reached them first, then the shape of him in the doorway.

Jed froze. The wolf-hide slung over the man's shoulders might as well have been a banner. Scars twisted his cheek. His grin showed too much tooth as he leaned on the counter.

"Mara! Got any loaves hot enough to burn the night in half?" His voice rasped through the room. "Or better yet, come to the Drunken Gull. Blackenguard's gathering there tonight. Captain himself's buying. We've coin enough to drown the city. Easy drink, easy women. Come by, I'll show you a better time than counting coppers."

Jed's claws bit the broom handle until wood splintered under his grip. His chest locked. That laugh cracked through him—smoke, stone, the moment the roof groaned.

Mara didn't flinch. Her eyes narrowed, knife-sharp. "You'll get your bread and nothing else."

The mercenary flipped a coin onto the counter, winked, and swaggered toward the door. "Don't say I never offered. Remember the name—Blackenguard always take care of their own."

His boots faded into the evening noise. The bell stilled.

Jed kept sweeping the same patch of floor, though it was already bare. His claws trembled, tail lashing low. The cloak under the hull would stink of men like him. Of fire. Of a scream he could not stop hearing.

Mara's gaze slid across him once—sharp, suspicious—then moved on.

When the last sack was stacked, Jed slipped into the night. Harbor lamps swung in the wind, light spilling over black water. The mercenary's voice still rang in his ears, dragging him back into the tunnels where smoke had swallowed everything he'd ever loved.

The Blackenguard were here. Drinking. Celebrating. Laughing.

Jed whispered Yarra's name, Kep's name. His claws dug grooves in the plank until his palms bled.

Not yet. But soon.

He would come for them.

Chapter 9

Rooftops and the Drunken Gull

J ed ran the whole way back to the water, a blur stitched from alleys and shadows, until the harbor reek found him. The broken skiff hunched on its side like a dead thing propped against the pilings. He dropped under its ribs and dragged his fingers through old nets until they caught the leather pouch of stones, the sling, Yarra's knife. He held the blade a heartbeat longer than necessary, thumb finding the nick near the hilt where she'd once slipped and laughed it off, her lip caught between her teeth. The memory hit hard enough to buckle him. He breathed through it, slow, and set the knife across his knees. The black fur cloak lay where he used it as bedding, but he left it. Its reek of smoke and sweat was no armor here.

"Tonight," he said, but only with his chest. His mouth didn't trust words.

The tide sucked at the pilings below, a wet, steady pull. Lanternlight from the quay dappled the black water in squares and streaks, as if someone had thrown coins into the sea and left them to drown. Jed slid out from under the hull and into those lights and then out of them again, keeping to the seams as he cut inland. He moved as he'd taught himself to move: test each cobble with his toes before committing weight, brush doorframes with his tail to feel for new splinters that meant a hinge had been replaced and might squeal, step over the places that remembered puddles even when they'd dried.

He was not strong. He was small. He let the city forget him as he crossed it.

Crates to cart. Shutters to climb. A drainpipe slick with someone's rinsed-off sins. He took the long route instead of the quick one, always angling toward the highest ledge, the narrowest span, the part of a roof that bowed inward rather than out so it would cradle rather than cast him. A cat hissed as he passed; he hissed back without thinking, low in his throat. The rooftops of Grayhaven were cold and close, a patchwork of slate and wood and patched tar. He moved across them on his fingertips and the pads of his feet, tail tight for balance, heart rattling fast in his chest until he slowed it again.

At the lip above Barrel Street he paused, letting the city wash past him: late carts rumbling on iron-bound wheels, a woman singing to herself because if she didn't sing she'd cry, a door slamming on a fight that hadn't finished. From up here the tavern signs rocked and banged where they hung. One creaked on its hinges louder than the others—the Drunken Gull—painted gull all beak and swagger, one wing out as if to slap someone.

Light pumped from the Gull's windows, gold and greasy. It threw the alley into a misery of shadow and glare. Heat rolled up from the roof, the tavern's sweat pushed out through the slats. Jed crawled belly-close to the eave and peered over, letting only one eye break the line. From this angle the windows were more gloss than picture, a smoked blur of shapes moving in and out of each other. A fiddle shrieked and then found something like a tune. Dice rattled hard against wood and a chorus of groans chased the sound. Tankards hit tabletops in a steady knock—knock that might as well have been hammers on a coffin.

He watched until his eyes stopped trying to make faces out of the blur. He watched the door instead. Men went in in twos and threes, shoulders touching, heads thrown back to drink from jugs before they even crossed the threshold. They wore wolf pelts—some whole, some only a strip stitched to a collar. Others wore black badges that caught the light. One had painted a white fang on his shield and it flashed whenever he turned. The company's name wasn't spoken, but it was written on their shoulders and steel.

He slid down the back of the roof where the moon didn't reach and found the alley that ran like a scar behind the Gull. It was narrow enough that he could press a shoulder into each wall and hold himself above the wet. The smell down there had layers—old ale, new piss, fried fat, something sweet and rotting that might have been fruit once. He kissed the knife's spine with his thumb the way Yarra had, more habit than belief, then tucked it flat under his arm where it wouldn't catch lanternlight. His sling he looped on his wrist, stones small enough to swallow.

He edged toward the side window. Moths battered themselves to death against it. The glass was smeared with handprints and smoke; inside, a barmaid shouldered through the crowd with a tray that had once been round and was all dings now. A man's hand hooked her waist. She shook him off with an elbow sharp enough to leave a bruise and didn't spill a drop. Another hand pinched at the string of her apron and undid it halfway because that's what hands do when they've been told they can. She said something—Jed read "no" on her mouth—and the men laughed as if they'd heard a joke and then told their own, louder.

"Another round for the captain!" a voice crowed. It carried like a man used to command. "Coin's fresh and thirsty!"

The cheer hit the rafters. Jed's chest went tight as a fist. His tail coiled around his ankle, squeezing until the ache snapped him back into the moment.

"Where's the captain?" someone yelled, already slurring. Dice knocked, skittered, clattered into a tankard and sent beer over a table's edge. "I won't drink to a captain who won't drink with his own."

"Aw, he said he's got to take a piss," another man answered, pitching his voice to be heard. "Man's got a bladder like a priest. Always draining, never smiling."

Laughter. It filled the room like smoke and made the rest hard to see. The barmaid swung her tray through it and someone's fingers—Jed felt them on his own skin—tried her again, slower, thumb drawing a circle where no circle was asked for. She set the tray down like she was slamming a door and the mugs rattled. The man who'd made the circle showed his teeth as if they were currency.

Jed's hand closed on the stone at his wrist until the edges dug. He imagined its weight crossing that glass, the bruise it would bloom on an unsuspecting skull,

41

the brief, clean music of bone giving. Veynar would see him then. Veynar would come. He eased the stone loose and dropped it back into the pouch. Not yet. Not at the window with a room full of mercenaries and the Watch two streets over rehearsing how fast they could arrive when told men with coin had been made unhappy.

Closer. The alley carried sound the way a den carries heat. He set his ear to the wall beneath the window and let the lies and boasts pour into him until they were indistinguishable.

"...smoked them out like rats. Gods, the screaming—" "—not rats. Smaller. Scrawny little lizards, that's all." "—you ever seen one up close? Like a child's skull stretched wrong—" "—captain did it right. Trap at the lower vents, fire at the top. Took the air and they were done before they knew to run—"

Jed didn't realize he'd climbed the brick until the brick bit his belly. He forced himself down again. Breathe. Count. Slow. If he went inside and cut one throat, five more would spill him, and there was no tunnel to vanish into here. Grayhaven wasn't his warren. He couldn't fight like it was. He had to be smarter than his bones wanted him to be.

He slid to the back corner, where the tavern wall met an older warehouse wall at a sloping joint of patched mortar and pride. There was a gutter there that had been hung wrong. It groaned like a tired man does when he lies down. He could go up it to the overhang above the back door and drop if he had to. If Veynar came that way. If.

He'd spent two nights before this one learning how the Watch staggered their lantern routes—when a man ducked off to the privy, when another took too long counting dice in a doorway. He had marked where shadows stretched longest. He knew this alley had its blind minute, and he was waiting in it.

A door banged open to his left and a man stumbled into the alley, head back to drink the last drop from a mug. He pitched the mug aside and it clanged against a barrel. He held himself enough to piss into the corner instead of on his boots and sighed as if relief were a song he'd been paid to sing. He hadn't pulled a sword, because he hadn't planned to need one. Jed let him finish. Let him sway. Let him tuck himself away like a boy.

Not him. Not yet. The captain.

Jed pressed his ear to the wood of the back door. It vibrated with the tavern's heart. The barmaid again, voice ragged: "I said no, Helmar. No! Get your hands off me." A hand slapped her—he heard the report—and the howl that followed was laughter. Someone said "easy now" and someone said "oh, she likes it rough then" and the laughter cracked wider. Jed saw Yarra's lip break on a fist that hadn't been meant for her. He saw Kep flinch and then pretend he hadn't, because he knew Jed would pretend he hadn't seen it if Kep pretended it first.

His throat made a noise he didn't recognize and he shut it down.

The alley's mouth burned brighter for a moment and dimmed. Watchmen. Lanterns. He stilled himself along the wall until the light slid off and kept sliding. If they'd looked into the alley they would have seen only a stack of barrels and a shape like a tarp that had come loose. He waited for their boots to lose their rhythm. He counted to twenty. Twenty again.

The door opened. Not the back door. The side one, where the privy path began. The smell that came with it killed the last of the moths at the window. A mercenary lurched out—broad shoulders, pelts stitched into his collar. Not the captain. Not Veynar. The man belched the kind of belch that made men laugh and women leave and then leaned on the wall to steady the world while it spun without him. He muttered something to it. The wall didn't answer. He blinked at the night and then back at himself, shrugged, and went to find the privy he'd already passed.

Jed's claws dug lines in mortar. Patience. Don't stab the second man and die. Don't waste your death on a man whose name no one will remember.

"Another round!" someone bellowed inside, as if the first ten hadn't taken. Dice again, the sound of a cup rattling bone. A chair broke. The roar that followed almost shook the window clean.

"Where's the captain, then?" came again, slurred—a man who'd lost two throws and wanted someone else to bleed for it. "Man said he'd drink. Man said he'd—"

"A piss," the earlier voice repeated, impatient now. "Took a piss. He'll be in when he's done measuring the night with it."

43

Mugs smashed for the joke. The barmaid's voice was smaller now, either from distance or because she had learned the shape of the room's attention and how to avoid it. Jed breathed through his teeth, slow.

Movement along the wall behind him. He couldn't name it at first. It wasn't a footstep or a dragged boot or a shoulder slammed into brick. It was the edited quiet that came when something larger than a man and smaller than a wagon wanted to be unnoticed but didn't care if he was heard in the last heartbeat of the person he'd found.

"Well now," said the thing that had made that quiet.

Jed's body recognized the voice the way a hunted animal recognizes a snare. His spine went cold and rigid. He turned because there was no other choice his neck would make.

Veynar stood less than a pace away. The wolf-pelt was heavier than Jed remembered, the fur clotted into ropes that threw shadows across his chest. Torchlight from the street picked out the nicked edges of the sword at his hip and the grease-shine on the leather of his gauntlets. The smile on his mouth was not wide. Wide smiles are for men who don't expect to win. His was a small thing, precise as a cut.

"Seems one of the rats slipped the net," Veynar said, as if remarking on the weather. His eyes didn't leave Jed's face. "No matter. I'll fix that."

Chapter 10

Chapter Ten — Cornered Rat

H e drew the sword without looking at it, a movement tidy as breath. Leather squeaked on the scabbard. The blade came out hungry.

Jed's hand had already gone to the knife. The sling slid to his palm with memory's ease. Stones waited in the pouch like thoughts that had been crowding his head all day, eager to be first. His tail came up off the cobbles as if it meant to make him look taller.

The alley tasted like iron.

He hissed once—because he couldn't not—all the way back in his throat where it hurt to keep it. Then he went at the man who had burned his home, who had smiled in the smoke while Kep coughed and coughed and then did not.

Jed struck first. He had to. If he waited for Veynar's blade to decide the moment, he'd never see the end of it. The sling whipped from his hand in a blur, a stone hissing against the wall as it found nothing but air. Veynar moved with the ease of someone who'd dodged arrows for half his life. The sword came up, kissed the light, and knocked the second stone aside before Jed even knew he'd loosed it.

"Quick little thing," Veynar said, voice calm as a knife laid flat. His eyes had the steadiness of a man watching a trapped animal twitch. "But still a rat."

Jed lunged low, knife flashing for the gap at the thigh. For one bright instant he thought he'd found it—thought he'd carve deep enough to win a sound besides that calm voice—but the pelt on Veynar's shoulder swung like a curtain, and the sword's pommel smashed Jed's wrist. The knife clattered. Pain shot up his arm, hot and white, threatening to empty him out.

He snatched the blade back before it skittered away and rolled to keep the captain's boots from stomping it flat. Veynar didn't rush. Two measured steps, patient—the way a hunter steps on a snared animal so it doesn't break the trap before dying.

Jed's tail whipped. The alley stank of piss and fried fat and old beer. He spat copper, hissed, and came again—sling strap tight around his hand as a garrote, knife feinting high before darting low. The edge bit the greave, sparked, slid. No blood. No cry. Only Veynar's boot hammering Jed's ribs and flinging him into the wall like he weighed less than a bundle of rags.

Grit ground between his teeth. The world rang. He rolled before the sword could finish the thought, claws cutting shallow furrows in wet cobble, scrambling not like a warrior but like a lizard refusing the heel.

The back door banged. "Captain?" a voice slurred from inside. "You still draining that thing?"

"Out here," Veynar called, as casual as telling a dog to heel. He didn't take his eyes off Jed. "Bring a light."

Boots scuffed. Two mercenaries spilled into the alley with torches, faces flushed with drink. Their laughter broke when they saw Jed crouched there, eyes wide in the lamplight.

"Well, shit," one muttered. "He's real."

The other grinned, ugly. "Rat-dragon." He tasted the word like he'd been starving for it. "Scales and all."

Veynar flicked his blade without looking. "Shut your mouths. Hold the light."

Jed moved before thought. He whipped the sling once, twice; a stone snapped the first torch into sparks. Darkness dropped like a curtain. The second torch flailed, tossing wild gold. Jed used that chaos, darted in, edge raking the back of a man's knuckles. The merc howled, dropped his light, and for a heartbeat the alley went nearly blind.

Jed dove for the gap, but Veynar's fist closed on the fur at Jed's scruff and hauled. Choking, he stabbed upward without looking, blade finding flesh—forearm—shallow, but enough to wet his hand. Veynar's hiss was more anger than pain. The sword answered in a backhand that kissed Jed's ribs, shallow but burning like poured iron.

More boots thundered. The alley narrowed with bodies. Jed felt the press of them before he saw steel.

"Alive," Veynar said, voice clipped now. "I want him alive."

Worse than death. Jed knew it. His chest squeezed; the edges of the world went dark. He had to leave now or be carried.

The second torch flared just enough to show a stack of barrels against the far wall. Jed flung his last stone hard into the lowest. Wood popped, brine burst, and the barrel above it toppled. Stinking fish liquor sluiced through boots, drawing curses. A merc slipped, smashed into another, both crashing against the wall. In the split of noise and bodies, Jed ran.

Not for the alley mouth—too many blades. He ran up. Claws and toes into mortar, tail balancing, ribs screaming. He climbed like the tunnels had taught him—straight vertical, trust the scars, trust the hands. Fingers clawed at his ankle; he kicked, felt a nose break. A sword struck sparks where his calf had been. He hauled himself over the ledge as the blade bit nothing but stone.

Rooftop wind hit him sharp and cold. He sprinted blind over shingles that cracked under his weight. Behind him, shouts tangled into one voice—Veynar's—cutting through clean: "Find the dirty rat. Finish the job!"

The words followed him across the roofs and into the dark.

Jed ran until the Drunken Gull's glow was a smear behind chimneys. His breath tore in his throat; every stride jarred the slash in his ribs. The rooftops pitched and bucked: tar patches slick as eels, shingles rotten to sponge, sudden gaps where a fire had eaten a house years ago and no one had bothered with new wood. He took one leap blind and landed on a window ledge, nails screaming against old paint, tail windmilling to keep him from pitching backward into open air. He clung, gulped air until black flecks receded, then crawled onto the next roof on elbows and knees like a child.

Below, the city shifted. Lanterns seemed closer now, voices louder. The Watch's rhythm changed, too—no longer the bored plod of men waiting for dawn, but an intent, quickened beat. Jed cut across a narrow gap into a warren of lower roofs where laundry lines webbed the night. A shirt slapped his snout; he bared his teeth at the ghost of a man who'd left it to dry.

"RAT! There!" a voice roared from the street.

He flattened. The shout came from behind and below; torchlight crawled up the walls like fire learning to climb. Jed slid belly-first down the slope of the roof and into the shadow of a chimney. He shut his mouth around his breath and tried to hear beyond his own pulse.

Boots. Many. A laugh too loud and wrong for the hour. Veynar's men, herding the Watch with coin and certainty. A dog's bark—high at first, then low as it caught a scent. Jed's skin tightened all over. He smelled himself: blood, salt, fur, old tar. He smeared a palm across the tar seam, then scrubbed that hand over his ribs and his face, making a mess of scents. He wished for fish guts and midden and had only what the roof gave him.

A door slammed open on the street below. A drunk staggered into the lamplight, swearing at his own feet. The dog lunged at him, all bark and teeth, and the handler cursed, yanking the line. "Not him, fool. The—"

Jed moved while the attention swerved. He cut across the roofline, dropped onto a balcony that was more rot than plank, felt it bow under him, and flung himself to the next roof as the balcony surrendered and fell in a sigh of old nails.

From somewhere left: "I see him!" From somewhere right: "Watch! Here! Here!"

He angled toward the water, toward the one map he knew by muscle and tide. The buildings thinned there; the wind came harder and colder, carrying the flat stink of the flats and the iron tang that never left. He slid down a slope and landed in the narrow seam between two warehouses, a grease-black lane where carts came to disappear from the tax man. He ran it heel–toe, heel–toe, because it had been cobbled by a man who hated anyone moving faster than a walk, and each stone jutted to punish the unwary.

A torch swung into the mouth of the lane. Jed went to ground behind a set of stacked fish crates, small as breath. The torch stopped. A Watch sergeant's voice:

"You—check behind the barrels. You—under the cart." A pause. "And if you see a kobold, don't play hero. Shout."

Boots advanced. A halberd butt rang as it knocked a wheel. Jed slid his tail tight along his thigh to keep it from betraying him with a twitch. He sank his claws into the crate slats and let splinters bite.

The halberd blade prodded the crate above his head. Wood groaned. He stilled so completely his chest hurt. A drip of brine ticked somewhere to his right—slow, steady, treacherous. The halberd moved on. The torch swung closer—close enough for warmth to touch his muzzle—then away, drawn by a shout from farther up the lane. "Sergeant! Blood and claw marks up the wall!"

The men ran toward the shout. The torch's glow went with them. Jed counted to ten in a language that was mostly numbers and scars. He rose, joints creaking like wet rope, and slipped the other way, toes finding the cracks, breath thin and quiet.

The river-mouth wind struck him clean when he cleared the warehouses. The docks lay like ribs, dark water between them. Lanterns swung at the ends of some; others sat blind, only the sea breathing beyond. Jed kept to the piles stacked like whale bones and the shadows they threw beneath the piers. The pilings were slick, but they were wood, and wood he knew. He moved from beam to beam with tail and fingers, belly inches above black tide, until the voices thinned into cold.

Far behind, a horn blew—short, answered, then again—and the answers moved away from him. Toward Barrel Street. Toward the Gull. Toward the noise Veynar had started and would not finish until dawn.

Jed crawled along the underside of a pier and dropped to the mudflats where the tide had pulled back. His feet sank cold. He didn't feel it. He ran along the waterline, bent double, gathering the stink of night. When at last the broken skiff hunched into view, it looked, for one terrible blink, like Veynar's pelt propped against the pilings. He almost turned and ran the other way.

He slid under the hull and didn't stop moving until the boards pressed his shoulders. The tide's breath filled the dark, wet and steady. He let it. He pressed his side where the cut had opened, hissed as the salt found it anyway, and pressed harder until the bleeding gave up.

He lay on his back on the cold planks and watched the ribs of the hull lean above him. They were crooked and wrong, like a mouth that could not close. He breathed until the world shrank to three facts: the pain in his side, the pain in his wrist, the pain where the pommel had caught his jaw. Then, carefully, he replaced each with another: the sound Veynar made when the knife bit forearm; the stumble when brine took his men; the single heartbeat of blind, perfect darkness when both torches died.

He should have died. He had not. He would not waste that mistake.

The city kept moving above the water—boots and horns and shouted orders scudding along the skin of night. In the dark under the hull, Jed said the names of his dead and held a stone in his palm and imagined it striking the smooth meat under Veynar's eye. He imagined the weight of the captain's sword in his own hand—not to swing, but to sell to buy oil and nails and the time it takes to become patient.

The tide climbed the pilings. The skiff creaked as if remembering seas. Jed shut his eyes only when the ache in his ribs softened from knife to dull rock. When he finally slept, it wasn't rest so much as a place without light where Veynar's voice still reached him: "Find the dirty rat. Finish the job."

He woke with the words in his mouth like a fishbone he could not spit.

He would teach the city to forget his shape again. He would make the Blackenguard speak softer. He would break what they leaned on—coin, drink, safety—and learn the turns of their hours. And when he came for Veynar again, it would not be with a rush and a hiss and a stone's prayer. It would be with a plan, patient as tide.

The hull's ribs held the dark. Somewhere out beyond the quay, a gull cried once and quieted, like a door shut gently. The Rat-Dragon listened to the sea breathe and turned his bleeding into a map.

Chapter 11

Beneath the Hull

J ed did not go to the docks.

He woke to daylight pooling unevenly under the upturned hull, a pale bruise of morning that made the tar-slick ribs of wood look like old bone. The pelt beneath him clung damp to his scales. When he shifted, the world tilted; pain ran a hot hook through his side and caught behind his ribs. He lay still and let the tide breathe for him. In. Out. The hull creaked as if remembering larger seas. Salt stung the cut along his flank. The skin there felt too tight, shiny with the effort of keeping him from falling open.

He reached for the rag he'd tied there in the dark and found it soaked, stiff as bark. He peeled it away with slow, careful fingers, and the wound spoke with a fresh wetness that made his stomach turn. Veynar had not gutted him, but the sword had carved deep, pouring fire into him and leaving it behind.

"Idiot," he rasped. His throat felt scraped raw, as if he'd swallowed smoke. "Idiot, idiot."

He tore a strip from the cloak's lining—a piece he would never have spared if the pain hadn't demanded it—and wound it tight around his ribs. His hands shook. Every loop made his vision spark and tighten. He bit the edge of the pelt and pulled until the cloth bound him, each wrap a new ring of pain, each knot a small surrender. When he was finished the world swam and the tide's breath had to teach his lungs all over again. The bandage slowed the bleeding but could not stop it.

He was thirsty. He crawled to the skiff's edge and dipped a cracked pot into the brackish pool that gathered under the pilings, lifted it, gagged at the taste of salt and old rope, drank anyway. The water slid down like knives. He thought of Yarra once and then not again because it widened the pain from a wound to an ocean.

"I should have waited," he said to the ribs of the hull. His voice sounded like someone else's—hoarse, thin, a man leaving a message for the person who would find his body by accident. "Should have watched. Should have been stone."

He saw himself again in the alley: the first rush, the hiss he hadn't meant to make, the knife finding only leather, the sword finding him. He had thought the small victories mattered. Two thugs in a side street. Another in the dark with his friend's laughter still on him. He had thought the stones in his sling turned him into something sharp, that practice could stand opposite a man like Veynar and pretend itself equal.

"Just a rat," he told the planks. "Just a rat with a knife."

The laugh that came out of him was small and ugly. It hurt his ribs.

He lay flat and watched dust move in the light. The dust moved slowly—small specks with their own tides. He matched his breathing to theirs. Outside, gulls worked the flats where the tide had gone off. From under the hull, their bodies were only white trowels moving the day around. Men's voices came and went—distant at first, then quieter, then gone. The docks had a rhythm in the mornings that could trick you into thinking there were rules: bells, ropes, curses, laughter, shoes dragging, someone singing off-key. Today the rhythm beat past him and left nothing but a slow, steady quiet broken by his breath and the creak of the hull.

He dozed and woke and dozed again. Hunger turned itself over and went back to sleep. Whenever he moved his side told him to stop. He counted the ribs he could see beneath his scales the way he had counted stones in the sling, as if one number could be a promise for the next. The light thinned and thickened. Ropes thumped as the tide changed. The world narrowed to the place where the bandage held.

Sometime after the light turned from iron to old honey, voices came that did not belong to the docks.

They came laughing.

"...told you he'll be skulking out here somewhere. They said he walks the beach like it owes him coin." "You sure you heard 'em right?" "Clean from the fishmonger. Says a scaly rat's been seen every night. Tall as my knee. Ugly as your mother."

Laughter. Boots on wet wood.

Jed's heart found its old bad rhythm and beat it fast.

He pressed himself into the nest of nets and broken rope and old tar the way a hatchling tries to hide under its own tail. The hull had never felt so thin. Each footstep outside came through the wood as clearly as if the man had put his heel on Jed's chest.

"Where?" another voice asked—bored, strong. He knew the shape of that kind of voice. A man who enjoyed the part where you begged him to listen and then did not.

"Past the pilings," the first said. "Old skiff turned roof. Little den under it. Said the rat goes in at dawn, out at night. Like a proper rat."

"Hear that?" a third voice—a man who would say anything if it made the others laugh. "Proper rat. Maybe he keeps a little broom. Sweeps his nest. Puts on a tiny apron."

"Maybe he wears your mother's dress," the second replied mildly. "This it?"

Jed didn't move. He let the tide breathe for him. He tried to feel small enough to slip between the splinters in the wood.

Fingers thudded along the hull, testing, tapping. Shadow slid over the thin light that filtered through the gaps. Someone squatted. He heard knees pop, smelled ale on breath that came through the boards in slow waves. The man leaned in close enough that Jed could hear him smile.

"Little rat," he crooned. "You in there?"

Silence. Salt. Jed kept his hands flat on the pelt. He imagined the knife in one and the sling in the other and then let the pictures go, because imagining wasn't the same as being able to hold them.

"Come on now," another said, knuckles rapping the hull like a knock at a door. "We only want a look. Captain says a rat survived. Captain wants him back. We'll be gentle."

"Nah," the third one said. "We won't." A thud—his boot—kicked the hull. Wood shuddered around Jed. Dust fell into his eyes. He didn't blink.

"Loosen it," the bored one said. "Doesn't matter if it breaks."

Boots scuffed to the far side. Hands worked at the hull's lip. The skiff had been dragged here in a storm and wedged fat between the pilings, weighted by old rope and silt. The men grunted. The hull jumped. Jed's stomach lurched as the world tilted. He clamped both arms over his ribs and pressed himself into the pelt. The hull rocked back and slammed into the pilings. The noise ran out into the water and came back smaller.

"Loosen it," the bored one said again.

"Come on out, little rat," the crooning voice sang, closer now, the sound of him moving up the hull like a man climbing a cradle. "Come out and we won't—" He paused, then laughed. "No, we will."

They started to break his home.

A boot heel stomped down between the ribs with a crack that sang in the wood. The boards above Jed's head shocked light through new lines. Another heel. Another. A pry bar bit somewhere, metal teeth digging at softened timber. The hull screamed a long, low scream like a ship dying slow. Nails popped. Dust fell in a steady dry rain. Jed shut his eyes and the dust found them anyway.

He curled tighter and held.

They taunted him as they worked. That was part of the fun. Promises said with a smile, like men telling each other about food.

"You'll like the captain," the crooner said. "He's kind. He keeps pets."

"He'll teach you to sing," another chimed. "What's a rat say? Squeak for us."

"Come out, I said."

A board above him gave. A hand came through the gap, groping. It closed on pelt and rope and found only trash. It withdrew with a curse. The pry bar bit deeper. The hull's belly tore another inch. Jed could see the outline of a face where shadows cut across the gap, could see the smudge of a tooth where the man was grinning at the prospect of finding something that bled under there.

Something in Jed uncoiled. It was not the part that planned, or counted, or mapped lantern swing against shadow. It was the part that had made him move in the warrens when the air turned black. The body that had carried Kep when reason said not to bother. It sent him forward through the tangle in a rush that pulled light into streaks. He didn't feel his ribs in the first three heartbeats. His hand found the knife because his hand knew where it lived even when his head couldn't think his own name.

He exploded out of the hole with a hiss no human throat could make. The man's face was right there, all grin and surprise. Jed did not go for the face. He went for the foot that held the world steady. The knife plunged down. Leather gave; meat gave; the blade bit bone with a hard, satisfying knock that traveled up Jed's arm. The man screamed. He reeled back, dragging the foot and the knife for a fraction of a second before the blade tore free and Jed was flying up through the wreckage and into blinding daylight.

"Shit—!" "Get him!"

He ran.

The beach pitch-tilted under him. The first three steps were perfect: light, low, the way he moved across roofs. The fourth sent a flare of white through his side so bright it erased the world. He stumbled, went to one knee, clawed at the sand, got up again because the voices behind him were already coming fast, laughing in the way men laugh when the outcome is certain and their blood is up for play.

He didn't know where he was going until the docks rose in front of him like a row of black teeth. He headed there because there were alleys there and not just open beach, because wood was kinder to climb than stone. His feet kicked up shells. The tide was out far enough that the smell of rot came up strong. He took it in through his mouth and let it sit there because his nose had too much to do.

"After him!" "Left—he's cutting left!"

A thrown rock bit his shoulder and spun away. He didn't look back. Looking back slowed your feet. He aimed at the gap between a bait shed and a net loft, hit it too fast, ricocheted off a post with his bad ribs and saw stars. He put a hand out, found a wall, pushed. The world tilted and hiccupped. His legs kept going because that's what he told them they were for.

He heard himself make a sound. Not a word. Something like a word's skeleton.

Sand gave to boards. The planks were slick, old fish oil caught in the grain. His toes gripped; his claws scraped. A boatman swore and yanked a crate out of the way. "Watch it—" then saw the men pounding after Jed and closed his mouth around even his own name. Jed took the narrowest seam between two stacks of barrels and the world of sound squeezed to fit: his breath, their breath, boots, the rattle of a spear haft against a crate.

The alleys here were little runnels carved by years of men with too much to do and not enough room. They kinked, narrowed, ducked under beams too low for a human to pass without bending. Jed scuttled under one that raked his back with splinters and used his tail to whip the beam as he went; it startled and swung, catching the first of his pursuers across the brow, and he went down cursing. The others leapt him. One kicked him for being in the way.

Blood warmed Jed's side and ran in a line that his own tail smeared without meaning to. He put the knife in his mouth because he needed both hands to take the next wall. He climbed, scrabbled, slipped on dried fish scales, got a hand on the sill of a window that had once held a flower pot and now held nothing but old dirt and a living cockroach. He moved over it, dropped into another seam. His ribs, already bruised and battered, gave a sound too much like a crack to be ignored. He told himself the sound belonged to the board he'd just landed on.

"Think he went in here!" "He's bleeding—look!"

The world narrowed again to a blind alley. It ended in a door with peeling paint and iron-banded hinges. No ladder. No low sill. No blessed gutter hung wrong. Just wood and a wall that rose straight and kissed a roof too high to take without a ladder and a miracle.

Jed stopped because there was nowhere left to go. He turned. The alley felt too narrow now, as if he had slipped into a pipe. He could smell himself, a child's smell—fear, salt, iron. The men coming smelled like different things: tar and ale and the animal that grows in a man when he knows he has someone smaller cornered.

His hand found the knife's hilt where it stuck between his teeth. He pulled it free. The blade looked shorter than it had in the dark. His tail coiled, the way it did when he wanted to make himself look taller. It didn't make him look taller. It made him steady.

"Come on then," he told the air. His voice wavered once and then remembered how not to. "Come on."

He would take as many as he could. He would go down with his teeth in someone's wrist.

Boots hammered the boards just around the bend. A voice, nearer now: "In there. I think he ducked in there. You to the left—cut him if he runs."

Jed set his feet. The alley narrowed everything into a single tomorrow. He breathed in and in. The cut along his side leaked. His head felt both too heavy and not there at all, as if he'd left it behind under the hull and was only now noticing.

The door behind him ripped open.

A hand like a hook went around his ribs and yanked him backward into a dark that smelled like pitch, hemp, and salt-damp wood. Jed's knife came up by reflex; it hit meat and stopped because the arm that held him was as big as a post and hard as one, too. The door slammed. A bolt slammed after it, iron into iron with a sound that sent the boards humming.

Outside, the boots thundered past. Inside, the dark swallowed his hiss.

Chapter 12

The Net Loft

"Easy," a voice said in his ear, low and urgent, the consonants softened by years at sea. "Easy, little brother. You're leaking all over my floor."

Jed twisted once, twice, and then stopped because the room moved with him and the arm under his chest did not. His head knocked into a shoulder that smelled of tar and smoke and sweat. The shoulder shifted to take his weight without complaint.

"Breathe," the voice said. A second hand—gentler—found the bandage and pressed where it needed to—not too hard. "Hold that."

The bolt settled in its brackets with a softer sound, as if hands were checking it twice. The touch came not from panic but from habit, the way a sailor runs fingers along knots even when he knows they'll hold. Someone—somewhere past the first man—moved soft-footed among hanging ropes and nets that whispered against each other like reeds. A lantern hissed to life, its wick coaxed small, only enough to paint a slice of light along stacks of coiled line and the edge of a bench scarred by years of knives. It found a face last—the grin familiar even tucked behind worry, the gray at the beard's edges shining like fishscale.

Brann.

Jed's knife dropped. The point kissed wood and lay there, stupid and small.

Brann put two fingers against Jed's cheek, steady as if testing his breath. "There you are," he said quietly, like he'd been calling across a long gap and had only now

59

got an answer. "Hells, but they worked you over. Mara's going to have words for you and for me if she sees the floor."

Voices outside swelled and receded, bouncing off alley walls, the hunt turning down another seam. The bolt held. Brann kept a palm on the wound, firm and competent; Jed breathed under it because Brann's hand told his body to do so. The lantern's thread of light trembled on a stir of air and showed Jed the place he'd been dragged into: some net loft or rope shed, never meant for hiding, but the walls and the bolt were enough for tonight. Hooks hung in rows. Tar seeped from old seams. A shelf held three clay cups and nothing that had ever been clean.

Brann eased him to a bench, never fully taking his hand off the wound. When he let go, he did it like a man who knows things break when you do it fast. He reached for a roll of linen, torn by hands that had torn linen for this purpose before. He soaked it from a jug that steamed faintly—water hot from somewhere—and cleaned the blood that had made Jed slick, his mouth pressed into a line when the cloth met the cut.

The world tunneled. Jed's eyes kept trying to close. He forced them open on Brann's face and found a patience there that men who live through storms learn or die without.

"Why," Jed said. The word came out in two breaths.

Brann glanced at the bolted door. The voices outside had thinned into insults aimed at empty air and at each other. Somewhere farther off, a man laughed the way men laugh when a thing is not yet funny but will be in the telling. Brann's mouth tightened before he smiled again.

"Because the sea's already had enough of you," he said simply. "And because I don't fancy the Blackenguard fishing in my yard."

He slid a folded wad of linen under the bandage he was winding, to make the pressure sit right. His hands were big and precise. Jed watched them, waiting for cruelty that didn't come.

"Be still now," Brann added. "You jump and I'll tie you like a hog. Not because I want to. Because you'll leave more of yourself on my floor."

Jed stared at the bolt. He could still hear Veynar's voice if he let himself: *Find the dirty rat. Finish the job.* He shut his eyes and for a blink the loft blurred away and the wolf pelt loomed, too close. Memory sharper than the ropes around him. He opened them again and saw only the lantern's small, stubborn light.

"I was an idiot," he said. The words were a whisper, but they had weight. "I thought—speed could make up for what I didn't have. I thought anger might carry me where my ribs and claws couldn't."

"Anger makes a poor ladder," Brann said without looking up. "It's a fine way to climb fast into a hole."

Jed swallowed. The cloth bit. He let it. The bench under him was rough and smelled of the sea. The room hummed with the life of old wood. He could feel splinters through his scales. He sucked air and felt it stick halfway.

"Don't talk yet," Brann said, gentle and implacable. "You've bled enough words for one night."

Outside, the hunt went past again, farther now, the sound of it thinning as if the men were taking their torches somewhere that would make a better story by morning. Boots rattled a ladder. A voice tried a door and found it barred and swore like a man insulted by wood. Brann didn't relax. Men like the Blackenguard had long shadows; even when their voices thinned, the danger never did.

Jed watched Brann's hands move, the way a man watches a hawk he's decided to trust because it hasn't taken his eye yet. He thought of Mara at her counter, weighing coin without looking at it, cutting everything she didn't need to hear away from the world with a sentence. He thought of Brann's laugh on the dock, loud enough to make gulls wheel, and of the way it had softened when Jed told him monsters lived in men.

"Rest," Brann said, when the bandage sat right and the bleeding slowed to a sulk. "You're safe here for the hour."

He sounded like a man who did not put too much hope into any single hour. Jed found comfort in that. He let his head go down to the wood. It was hard and it smelled like a thousand dead fish and it was the best thing he'd ever put his face on.

"Just a rat," he whispered, not sure if he spoke in Common or in the little language he'd kept for his family. "Just a rat."

61

"Maybe," Brann said. The lantern light made his eyes look younger than his beard. "But even rats have teeth. And sense enough to wait till the cat blinks."

He rose, checked the bolt again—slow, habitual—and set himself on a crate opposite, elbows on knees, watching the door as if watching a squall roll in. He kept his body between Jed and the street. He kept himself loose, as if a fight could come through wood and he would have to turn his joints into rope to meet it.

Jed's eyes slid shut. In the dark inside his own head he saw the alley again, the blue edge of Veynar's blade, the black edge of the pelt. He smelled the privy and the fried fat and the iron in his own blood. He waited for the panic to seize his chest the way it had in the shadows when the sword took him, but it didn't. The tightness that had been a fist loosened by fingers. He realized, with the kind of surprise that makes a body feel its own spine, that he was not alone.

The door did not move. The night went on. The tide crept back up the pilings. Jed breathed to its count and let the line between waking and sleep blur.

When the world came back to him again it did it in pieces: the scratch of rope shifting on a hook, the hiss of the lantern dropping a notch, the murmur of Brann's voice in the next room saying something soothing to someone who wasn't there, then the simple weight of his own body on the bench. He tasted salt. He tasted copper. He tasted the promise of air that was not filled with smoke.

He opened his eyes. Brann was where he had been, but more tired now, as if watching the door had aged him a year in an hour. He caught Jed looking and smiled like a man caught singing to himself.

"Next time," Brann said softly, "you let me know before you take on a captain, eh?"

Jed's mouth worked. It remembered how to lift at one corner and did, barely. "Next time," he said, and it was so much like a lie he almost laughed. The laugh would have hurt. He let it sit in his chest like a warm stone instead.

Outside, the mercenaries' voices had thinned to the occasional shout—angry now, tired, covering their failure with bluster. The Watch's horns sounded once, a tired note, and went quiet. Boats knocked soft against their ropes. Somewhere a gull gave one last call and then folded its head into its wing.

Jed let the quiet take him. He held on to the shape of this room in his mind even as it softened at the edges: bolt, rope, bench, lantern. A man between him and the door. He slid toward the dark and didn't fight it. The last thing that reached him across that dark wasn't Veynar's voice. It was Brann's, speaking low, because some men learn to talk to storms and to wounded things the same way.

"Sleep, little brother."

Jed did.

Chapter 13

Chapter Thirteen — Bread and Ash

When Jed woke, the light was already high. Not the thin flicker of dawn he'd grown used to stealing, but the broad glow of a sun well past morning. He blinked against it, the beams falling through a crooked shutter into the small room. His body ached everywhere. His ribs felt packed with glass, each breath sharp enough to draw water to his eyes.

On the table by the bed sat half a loaf of bread, its crust browned, its steam faint but real. Jed's stomach twisted at the smell. He knew that smell—Mara's shop.

He tried to rise and nearly toppled back, clutching at his bandaged side. The bandage was new, clean linen instead of the filthy wrap he'd tied himself the night before. Someone had seen him near death and hadn't left him in the gutter.

A shadow moved.

"Stay put, scales," came Brann's voice. The big man ducked into the room, carrying a mug of something that steamed. His hair was sweat-tangled, his shirt still dusted with salt as if he'd come straight off the docks. He set the mug down and crossed to the bed.

"You're lucky," he said, dragging a chair across the floorboards with one arm. "Mara near tore my ears off this morning when you didn't show. I was halfway to thinking you'd skipped town. Then word comes 'round that someone tried to put a knife in the Blackenguard captain. Guess who fits the bill?" He gave Jed a long, knowing look before he sat and straddled the chair backward, arms folded across its back.

Jed lowered his eyes. His claws dug at the blanket.

Brann sighed, then picked up the bread and tore it in half, pressing the softer piece into Jed's hands. "Eat before it cools."

Jed hesitated, then took a bite. The taste almost undid him—the warmth, the faint salt in the crust. He remembered Yarra's laugh as she bartered for loaves, Kep's small fingers pulling at the bread before it cooled. His throat locked tight.

Brann studied him a moment longer, then leaned forward. "So. Out with it. No more dancing. You've been skulking 'round the docks with shadows in your eyes and I'm about tired of guessing. Who are you really, and what in the drowned hell did you think you were doing tangling with the Blackenguard captain?"

Jed looked down at the crust in his hands. He could lie. Pretend again that he was just another stray scale looking for coin. But what did he have left to protect? His home was ash. His wife. His son. Gone. Only the memory remained, and even that was rotting inside him like an old wound.

His claws tightened until the bread tore. He whispered, voice raw, "It was him."

Brann tilted his head. "Who?"

Jed lifted his eyes, pale and bloodshot, fixed them on Brann. "Veynar. The Blackenguard captain. He burned the warrens. My clan. My...my family." His voice cracked on the last word. He forced the rest out in a rush before it drowned him. "He wore the wolf pelt that night. I remember him—torch in one hand, sword in the other, shouting orders like it was nothing but work. Smoke everywhere. Screams. The roof fell in. I was carrying my son when—when—"

He choked, claws curling against his chest as if he still held the boy there. His breath rattled.

Brann's face hardened, but he didn't interrupt. He let Jed fight the words out.

"When I stood again, my arms were empty. Yarra—my mate—she was still behind me. Kep—my son—he was gone. Buried. And Veynar smiled when he saw me. Like he was stamping a pest under his boot."

Jed pressed his palms to his face. The bread tumbled to the floor. "They all died. Every one. And I lived. For what? To crawl through gutters and steal scraps like some rat? He took everything. Everything. I thought—" His voice faltered. "I thought if I could put a knife in him, it would mean something. That maybe their spirits would rest. But I was a fool. He broke me like a twig. If not for luck, I'd be ash with them."

The room held only Jed's ragged breaths. The bread's steam faded into the air.

Brann sat very still. His hand went to his beard, tugging once, then fell. He stood slowly, pacing to the window. The boards creaked under his weight. For a long time, he said nothing. Jed half-expected him to walk out, to tell Mara there was a killer under her roof.

But Brann turned back, eyes sharper than Jed had ever seen. "I'll be honest, scales. That's one hell of a tale. If I hadn't heard the Blackenguard bragging myself, I'd call it madness. But..." He let out a rough breath. "I believe you. Gods curse me, but I do."

Jed blinked at him, stunned.

Brann came back to the chair, leaned his forearms on it again. "I've seen Veynar's kind. He and his dogs make a living butchering folk like you—folk who never did a thing but breathe wrong near the city walls. Last time he and his pack strutted down to the docks, we made it clear they weren't welcome. That was years back. Seems the city keeps calling them anyway."

His jaw tightened. "You're right to hate him. No shame in that. But you? Running at him alone, half-healed, with nothing but a knife? That's suicide, not vengeance."

Jed stared at the floorboards. The shame cut worse than his wounds.

Brann's voice softened. "Listen. Heal first. Think it over after. You tell me what you want to do, and I'll stand with you. Might be we can't bring down the Blackenguard and their captain outright, but there are more ways to bring down a wolf than running at its teeth. You hear me?"

Jed swallowed hard. He didn't trust his voice, so he only nodded.

Brann slapped the back of the chair and stood, stretching his broad shoulders. "Good. Then here's how it goes: you stay here till you can walk straight. I'll mend your tattered sails and keep Mara off your tail. And when this storm blows over, you and me are sitting down with a bottle, man to…kobold. Doesn't matter. We'll drink like equals."

For the first time since the warrens, Jed felt something stir in his chest that wasn't grief or rage. It wasn't trust—not yet—but it was close.

He lay back against the pillow, clutching what remained of the bread, and closed his eyes. For a moment, he let himself imagine Kep's small hand in his.

Outside, the gulls cried. Inside, Brann's boots thudded on the stairs. Jed whispered into the empty room:

"Not a rat. Not anymore."

Chapter 14

Three Days Still

Time crawled like a wounded thing.

The shed smelled of hemp and tar, but it held more than rope. Jed lay on the sailor's cot Brann had wedged against the wall—linen rough, straw crinkling under him. An upturned crate served as a table beside it, scarred and holding whatever Brann set down last: a crust of bread, a cheap knife, the heel of a bottle. A squat iron stove crouched in the corner with a crate of timber scraps stacked beside it; when the wind nosed under the door, the stove ticked, as if remembering heat. A narrow cabinet leaned against the back wall—Brann's bottles—and even with the door latched the breath of spirits hung in the wood.

Rope still ruled the place. Bowlines big as his head. Neat, proud coils like sleeping snakes. Tar-dark hawsers that shed grit if you dragged a palm across them. Nets hung to dry, whispering to one another when the draft turned.

He learned the shed by touch and sound. Which creak belonged to the front hinge and which to the back. Where the light found its way in through the crooked shutter when the sun shifted over the river mouth. How Brann's boots carried differently when he moved in the other room—the one with the sailor's bed he'd made from crates, linen, and straw. How pain ran its tide through a body: swelling near noon, easing a little after dusk, teaching a rib cage to breathe around places that didn't want moving.

When he tried to stand the first time, white burned through him and he sat down fast. Two ribs had gone in the alley. The linen binding Brann had wrapped him in held them where they belonged, but they hated him for it. The sword-cut along his flank had turned angrier on the second day—wet, then itching when it dried. He kept his claws off. He'd earned it. It could itch.

Brann came and went in the rhythm of Grayhaven. He'd stomp in smelling of salt and smoke, shoulder out of a coil of line, loosen the binding with careful hands and a muttered "easy, now." Sometimes he brought a pan to the little stove and coaxed a thin broth out of an onion and a stale heel; sometimes he poured hot water from a kettle that steamed and cleaned the wound in slow presses. He talked the way sailors do, like a net cast to see what it brings back: a winter squall that took three masts and a man too proud to lash himself to the rail; a captain who swore the sea sang names to him and then married a baker and never looked east again; a run south where the air tasted like peaches and iron. Sometimes he sang half a work-song into his teeth while he worked. Sometimes he let the quiet sit and the stove tick and the tide count breaths for both of them.

By the third day, the walls pressed close. The smell of hemp and tar had sunk into his scales, into the linen, into his dreams. He wanted to move—climb—find a roofline and feel slate under his palms, remember the body he'd had before a blade bit it. He braced to stand, and the room tilted; the cut along his side flared hot and red and sent him back to the cot, breath broken wrong. He lay and counted the strands in the nearest coil until the need to run shrank to something he could swallow.

So he did the thing Brann told him to do. He thought.

He sifted the last week grain by grain: the woman and her boy in the alley; copper on his tongue; the two men who had turned into bodies because he'd decided to practice on flesh; the glow of the Drunken Gull; voices that laughed at other people's fear; Veynar's voice inches from his spine; the wrong weight of that smile. He ran the night until remembering hurt less than denying it. He had stepped out of shadow to meet a sword that belonged to a man who did not doubt. He'd let easy kills teach him the wrong lesson.

The fourth morning came in thin and cold. Jed was half-asleep, clammy sweat on his neck, when the latch clacked and voices shoved the air ahead of them—low and hard, two people used to arguing while working.

"—and I said if you'd tied off the far side, the pressure would've—"

"The pressure would've nothing if you'd had the sense to—"

Mara shouldered through with her elbows already out, hair stabbed through a knot, a basket bumping her hip. Her eyes found Jed, slid to the bandage, to the way he hunched trying not to move. She reached back without looking and smacked Brann in the back of the head with two fingers.

"Ow," Brann said, wounded in pride more than anything, ducking in after her with a bottle fished from his cabinet.

"You tied him like a herring," Mara snapped, crossing to the cot. "No wonder he looks like death teaching itself to stand up." She put the basket on the crate table with a thump, leaned over the binding and clicked her tongue like the knot had insulted her. "How can a man wrap a rope to hold a storm and still fail a strip of linen?"

"In my defense," Brann said, sheepish, "he was bleeding all over me, and he hisses when you touch him."

"Because you poke the wound like a boy prodding a crab," Mara muttered. She pinched the knot free with quick fingers, and the binding sighed loose. Cold air touched the cut. Jed's skin breathed even though the next breath hurt.

Brann edged nearer with the bottle. Mara took it from his hand without looking, flicked him a glance sharp enough to cut line when he started to protest, and he shut his mouth like a man who'd just lost an argument with weather. She soaked a rag with spirits, wrung it once, and dabbed the raw seam.

Lightning. Jed's back arched without his say-so; every muscle from ribs to tail went iron. The shed narrowed to the wet fire on his skin. He hissed, not out of anger but because the body chose a noise that might keep it together.

"Smarts, doesn't it?" Mara said, unsympathetic and not unkind. "If there's one thing a sailor's drink is good for, it's numbing a fool who didn't die when he tried." She tilted her head, studying the edge of the cut like a seamstress buying cloth. "Hold still."

71

Her hand was steady as she stitched. Too steady for only a baker's. Jed watched her fingers move and she caught him watching.

"Don't gawp. You're not the first fool I've sewn, just the scaliest."

Brann chuckled into his knuckles. "She's underselling herself. Used to doctor a crew, our Mara. Half the Greenfin owes their hides to that needle."

Mara cut him a look and the chuckle died. "A long time ago," she said.

Jed winced as the thread tugged. "Why'd you stop?"

Her mouth pressed thin. She tied off the stitch, reached for more spirits. "My husband," she said at last. "Sailor. Handsome as sin and twice as daft. Saved coin for a shop by the docks. 'Bread,' he said. 'Fresh bread instead of hardtack.' Wanted something honest. His." She dabbed the wound; he hissed; she ignored it. "So I left the sea. Traded storms and blood for flour. Thought I'd have forever to regret it. He—" She paused, needle still. "He died a few years back. Just me now. Me and the ovens."

Brann's voice gentled. "Could've gone back aboard. Chose not to. Keeps the quay fed. Keeps him here."

Mara pulled the last stitch tight, snapped the thread, and sat back. "Don't mistake me for sentimental. A man's dream doesn't need love to keep breathing. Just stubborn hands." She flexed hers once. "Lucky for him, I've got two."

Brann hauled a chair over and swung it backward, leaning his arms on the back. "Right," he said. "Have you come to a decision about what you're going to do?" He scratched his head with the bottle neck; Mara pinched his ear for trying to do both things at once.

Mara cleared her throat when Jed didn't answer fast. He realized he was staring at the needle like it might bite again.

Brann filled the space. "I told Mara your story," he said, eyes flicking to the floorboards as if checking a friend before speaking a man's secrets. "All of it. Don't lock up. She's a soul you can trust. Bark's worse than bite." He rubbed the ear she'd twisted. "Only a little worse."

Mara snorted. "My bite is exactly as bad as it should be." She tipped her chin at Jed. "Half in the grave or not, you need to hear something and I'm the one to say it. There's a bounty on your head."

The shed changed shape. The words lived in it now.

She went on, flat. "Blackenguard took it to the Watch. They gave your shadow a name—Rat-Dragon." Her mouth twisted. "Stupid name. Doesn't matter. The posters don't need clever. Anyone brings you in breathing gets coin. More if they keep quiet about it."

Brann's bottle stopped short of his mouth. He looked at Jed, and the easy lines he kept for jokes slid off his face.

Mara opened her hands, palms up—laying facts on his blanket. "The longer you lie here, the longer you put Brann and me in danger. The Blackenguard want your head for sport; the Watch want it for order. Best bet is to heal and go. Find a smaller harbor. A kinder one." She huffed through her nose. "But men don't listen to reason. Neither do kobolds."

Brann made a small noise that sounded like a protest and a laugh got tangled up. Mara ignored it. She set bread and a hard wedge of cheese on the crate table and put Brann's little rope-knife beside them. "Eat," she said, to keep his hands busy while his head churned.

Jed stared at the bread. He pictured leaving: slipping through alleys that didn't know his shape yet; finding a river mouth with nothing but fish and clean wind; a life where no one spoke Yarra's name. He let the picture stand for a heartbeat and then knocked it down.

He chewed. It tasted like nothing. "I can't face him like that again," he said at last. The shed had settled enough for his voice to come back to him. "Not with a rush. Not alone in a bright alley. I'm not...that." The last word came small; he swallowed it. "But the man shouldn't get to smile about what he did. My clan—" His throat closed. He forced it open. "—my family demand a debt paid."

He lifted his eyes to Mara, because it hurt less than looking at Brann's gentleness. "I'm grateful for what you've done. I can't promise it wasn't for naught."

Brann huffed, a sound that had laughter without mockery. He jerked his chin at Mara. "Told you. Scales or not, he's a man."

Mara rolled her eyes like a woman who'd seen three wars and five men cry in her shop. "Gods curse the lot of you. Doesn't matter the species—you're built with half a brain and a full appetite for trouble." She leaned until her shadow touched

73

Jed's toes. "If you insist on this fool's errand, you'll do it the sensible way, which means listening for once in your scaled life." She jerked her head at Brann. "And to him. Old Brann will teach you a few tricks from his roguish days he pretends he never had."

Brann tried to look offended and failed. "Roguish? I was an honest sailor."

"You were a dock thief with a good smile," Mara said. Then, ticking points off on blunt fingers: "You need soft feet. Patience. Learn the Watch's map—their lantern swings, where they pause to scratch, which alleys swallow sound. Learn when to cut and when to leave a man bleeding. If you must leave a mark, leave it where it buys you three days' grace instead of three minutes." Her eyes held him steady. "You think you're the only one who's lost something? The city's full of ghosts. You want justice, be the draft that makes doors squeak and men look away without knowing why."

Brann lifted the bottle in salute and set it down without drinking. He pointed at the binding. "And listen to your ribs. Walk bent a week; live another month. Breathe shallow; learn to move your shoulders without your chest. Practice with the sling against pilings till you can hit a knot you can't see."

Mara rose, wiped her hands on her apron like the work had left something soap wouldn't take, and tucked needle and thread back in the basket. "Three days," she said. "No roofs. No alleys. Let those stitches settle. After that, if you're still set on getting yourself killed, you'll start by not getting yourself killed. You'll watch. Listen. Learn where the Blackenguard captain drinks that isn't the Gull—he'll change habits now he knows a rat watches. Learn who brings him messages. Which men he trusts and which he keeps for pretty noise. Learn how to make men like that step wrong without putting your throat under their boots."

She nodded at the door. "Don't use the same path twice. Let me and Brann be seen when you're elsewhere. We'll make a little noise for you. Enough to throw shadow, not enough to catch any."

Jed looked at the two of them: the woman who'd once called him cheap labor and now stitched him neat as a sail; the big man who dragged him out of a mouth that would've closed. The words for the heat in his chest didn't come. He bowed his head instead. That he could still do without breaking.

"I'll listen," he said. "I'll learn. I'll be patient."

Mara grunted—her yes. Brann scraped his chair back, clapped his hands once like sealing a deal with the air. "Good. First lesson starts when you can walk from here to that door without cursing your mother."

"I don't—" Jed began.

"Then curse mine," Brann said. "She can take it."

Mara snorted. "Your mother could take a hurricane and briefly consider it weather." She stooped for a thread-end she'd dropped and missed it; Brann bent and picked it up, because for all his bulk he had careful fingers. "Eat," she told Jed, softer now. "Sleep. Listen to the dock. It tells you who's afraid. Who's lying. The city's a mouth that never shuts; you only have to learn which teeth not to get cut on."

They left him the rest of the bread and the bottle with its lip wiped clean. Brann ducked into the other room first; Mara followed, pausing like she might tack one more warning onto him. She didn't. She set the latch just-so—firm, not loud. Their absence held for a breath, then the tide's breath came back in.

Jed lay still and let the careful stitches tug. He listened. Rope against wood. A gull finding a crab. A man deciding not to argue with his wife today. Farther, a watchman's lantern scraping its hinge—a small sound that said he always swung a little too high. The stove clicked in the draft. In the other room, Brann's bed creaked once as he sat to pull off his boots.

Jed ate. He slept. When he dreamed, the smoke was thinner. When he woke, the hurt was still there, but it had edges he could map. He pressed his palm against the bandage—not to stop anything, only to know where he began and ended. He was a kobold in a human city with a price on his head and two people who had decided not to sell him. He would be worthy of that mistake.

He let the tide count his breaths. Outside, two voices already bickered down the alley—one deep and rough as rope, one sharp as a needle—and to his surprise the sound made his ribs hurt less.

Three days. Then he would go still as a noose and learn how to make a wolf miss.

Chapter 15

How Days Turned

Jed healed slow. Days passed in a haze of pain, the air of the dockside shed thick with tar and damp rope. Brann drifted in and out like tidewater—sometimes with food, sometimes with a bottle, always with a story. He spoke of storms and ships, of sharks and barrels of fish, of sailors who laughed too long at their own luck. Jed listened because it kept the silence from pressing too hard.

But the bounty gnawed. "Rat-Dragon." A joke painted in rough ink, but one that carried knives. He could feel it whispering through Grayhaven's alleys even here, tucked under Brann's patched roof.

By the third day, the walls pressed close. The smell of hemp and stale liquor clung to his scales and bandages. He longed for open air, for rooftops, for the old rhythm of running, but each time he shifted, his ribs jabbed him clean through. He lay still, counted the cracks in the planks above him, and let the ache remind him what Veynar had taken.

On the fifth morning, Brann came with bread under his arm, hair damp with river spray. He sat on the edge of a crate and studied Jed the way a man studies weather, waiting to see which way it will break.

"You look like a gull locked in a hold," Brann said. "Pacing inside your own skull. If you're set on tangling with wolves, you'll need more than teeth and a sling." His voice dropped. "Mercs are sniffing around. They've got coin in the

Watch's pockets. The city doesn't care who gets cut, so long as the ledgers stay fat. If you mean to live, you need teaching."

Jed bristled. "I've fought before. My clan—"

"Your clan is ash," Brann said, not unkind. "This is Grayhaven. Rules change here. Small can live, but only if it learns how to slip."

And so it began.

The warehouse Brann chose was a forgotten place near the river mouth, its beams veiled with cobwebs, its air sour with rot and sawdust. Tools lay rusting in corners like bones. Brann laid a broad palm against a post as if it were kin. "My father built ships here. I keep it standing because a man likes four walls of his own. Now you'll use them to bleed in."

Jed's first lessons were light—steps, breath, weight. Brann showed him how to roll onto the balls of his feet, how to move shoulders loose so nails in the beams stayed quiet. For all his size the sailor slipped through shadow with a grace Jed wouldn't have believed if he hadn't seen it. Jed tried to follow, but every stumble rattled his ribs and earned a hiss he couldn't choke down. Brann only laughed. "You sound like a crate of pots, friend. Loosen up. You're bone, not water."

Knives came next. Brann showed him the throw—snap of wrist, point before spin. Jed's first blade bounced off timber and clattered across the floor. His claws tightened. He tried again. By the time sweat dampened his scales and his arms shook, one finally stuck. Brann grinned wide. "There it is. Rat's learning to bite from a distance."

Jed still kept the sling. Brann waved it off as a boy's toy, but Jed worked it when the sailor's back was turned—stones striking pilings, knots in the beams—a rhythm that felt like home. Brann didn't press the point.

Later came the crossbow—an old piece Brann pulled from under canvas, wood polished smooth by years of hands. "Equalizer," Brann called it. "Any fool can pull a trigger, but patience makes the bolt land." Jed listened. Patience was the one thing his ribs had already been teaching.

When Brann's work pulled him away, Mara took his place. Her lessons cut sharper. She taught him the city's map: which streets the Watch patrolled thick, which alleys swallowed noise, which lantern swings marked a patrol change. She drove it into him until his skull ached. "Every step's a choice," she snapped. "Waste one, and you waste blood." When he answered slow, she cuffed him on the back of the head. "Use that skull for more than pity."

Jed bore it. Sometimes the sharpness lit heat in his throat, but her fire reminded him of Yarra, and he let it burn. Mara's hands were quicker than Brann's and steadier; her stitches had already proved as much. She never spoke of her past unless Brann teased it out, and then it came with teeth. Ship's doctor, once. Jed filed it away with the rest of the city's scars.

Grayhaven itself showed him the rest. He heard it in Brann's mutters, in Mara's blunt warnings, in the posters nailed to wharf beams. The mercenary guilds lined the Watch's purses; the Watch lined the council's. "Law here's written in ledgers, not ink," Brann said once, tearing down a poster before Jed could study the rough snout sketched on it. Mara only added, "The city eats so long as it's fed. Doesn't matter if it's bread or blood."

The days blurred. His ribs still ached, stitches still pulled, but his feet grew quieter, his knives found timber more often than floor, and the crossbow's bolt began to strike true. Mara taught him locks and holds—how to twist a wrist or draw breath from a chest bigger than his own. He bruised, but she nodded once when he used her own lesson to put her flat on the boards. "Not hopeless," she said, and turned back to her bread.

Evenings ended with stew, cheap wine, and Brann's stories. Mara rolled her eyes; Jed listened. One night, when she muttered that he wasn't a complete idiot, he let out a thin smile without meaning to. The room stilled. Brann leaned back with mock awe.

"Well I'll be," he said. "The rat can smile. Careful with that—show fewer teeth, you'll scare fewer gulls."

Mara smacked his shoulder, but the corner of her mouth twitched.

For the first time since the smoke and screams of the warrens, Jed felt something loosen in his chest. Not trust. Not safety. But close.

Still, the bounty hung, and Veynar's laugh came back each night. He knew this training—this borrowed reprieve—was not escape. It was a whetstone. And one day soon, the blade it sharpened would meet the man in the wolf pelt.

Chapter 16

The First Mark

The day after Mara had stitched him for the last time, Jed found himself staring at the map spread across the table, its parchment smudged with oil from Brann's fingers and marked with Mara's sharp handwriting. He traced the ink lines with one claw. Grayhaven sprawled like a nest tipped sideways, streets curling off the main avenues into knots of alleys and blind corners. He knew the warrens of his people better than the bones of his own hands, but this city was still foreign—its smell, its voices, its order and disorder. Mara had drilled him on it night after night, and now the streets lived in his head almost as much as the tunnels of home.

Three taverns. That's what the gossip said. Blackenguard men liked to drink, and they liked to do it near their den. One in the Merchant Square, another by the docks, a third on the far side of the city. He tapped the square first. No. The Watch was thick there, patrols doubled during festivals and quarter days. He'd already seen the Watch lean on tavernkeepers for "fees," eyes blind as mercs swaggered past with coin heavy in their hands. Jed had no interest in dying under a gallows for the price of another man's bribe.

The docks? He let out a bitter breath. He still tasted blood when he remembered that night. He wasn't going back to that tavern unless he was dragging Veynar out of it by the throat.

That left the third. Not as close, but that was the point. Buildings pressed tight there, stacked like crates. Shadows layered over shadows. A place to hide; a place to strike. Jed heard Mara's voice at the back of his skull: smart is surviving, fool is dead. For once, he thought, she might even approve.

He leaned back in the chair, wincing as his ribs caught. Each movement reminded him of that mistake—thinking he could bring down Veynar with nothing but fury and a knife. He pressed a hand against the bandage, breathing steady until the pain settled.

His eyes drifted to the crossbow lying across the table. Brann's gift. A real weapon, not the sling of a hatchling. He ran a claw along the stock, feeling the grooves worn smooth by other hands. Beside it lay the bolts, their tips darkened with blotfish poison. Mara's idea. He remembered her frown as she dabbed the venom on with a rag. "It won't kill a man," she'd said, "but he'll wish it did. Handle careless, and I'll be stitching more than ribs." Then she'd smacked his knuckles when he reached for one before it dried.

Now, as the late sun slanted through the shutters, he lifted one bolt carefully, turning it in the light. Not enough to kill, but enough to drop a man to his knees. Enough to remind Blackenguard's pack that they bled like anyone else.

He reached for Brann's cabinet and pulled out a half-empty jug. Brann would grumble later, but the man had a sailor's stomach—he'd never miss it. Jed poured a swallow into a chipped cup. It burned going down, rough and sour, but the tremor in his hands eased. Not courage, but steadiness.

"Eye for an eye," he whispered, the words rasping in the quiet. It was what his clan believed. What his father had told him when the humans first raided their outer warrens. What Kep had whispered the night they fled together, their son clutched between them. Jed shut his eyes and saw his boy's face again, half-formed in memory, half-burned in smoke. The vow locked tight in his chest.

He gathered the bolts, slid them into the quiver, checked the strap on the crossbow. Then he pulled the cloak Mara had made from its peg—dark wool, dyed uneven but good enough to break his outline in shadow. She'd worked the seams with a surgeon's patience, muttering about wasted evenings and fools' errands, but she'd finished it all the same. He swung it around his shoulders and felt safer under the weight.

The city would not see a kobold tonight. It would see a shadow.

Jed set everything in place on the table and lowered himself onto the cot. He would need strength when night fell. He told himself he'd only rest his eyes. But sleep came fast, and in dreams he was back in the warrens, smoke crawling through the tunnels, his son slipping from his arms into fire. He woke with a sharp breath, ribs aching, throat raw. Darkness had fallen.

He lit no lamp. Instead, he fastened his belt, checked the crossbow again, and pulled the cloak hood low. Outside, the dockside street was quiet except for gulls squabbling over fish guts and the splash of tide against stone.

Jed moved.

He stuck to alleys first, slipping past the glow of lanterns where watchmen leaned on their spears, bored but sharp-eyed. Brann's lessons whispered in his ears: don't fight the light—use it. Step where they don't look. Wait for the cough, the turn of the head, then move. He heard two watchmen grumble as he passed unseen—"coin keeps the peace better than steel," one muttered, and the other laughed, "aye, so long as it's Blackenguard coin." Jed's claws dug his palm until it hurt.

He crossed streets unseen, roof to roof when he could, until the stink of pitch smoke and spilled ale rose up to meet him.

The tavern sat squat at a corner, its sign swinging on rusted chains. He perched above it, crouched between two chimneys for cover—the door below and right, a streetlamp throwing a bright oval of light ten paces out. From here he could count by shape in the window-glow: seven, maybe eight inside. He needed only one.

The door banged open.

A Blackenguard stumbled into the street—wolf-badge half undone, voice too big. He pissed in the lamplight, then lurched toward the dark seam between lamps, swagger loose and loud.

Jed settled the crossbow on the parapet. Range: eighteen paces. Crosswind: none. Sight on the meaty ridge above the bicep—muscle, not vitals. He exhaled. Squeezed.

Thrum.

The bolt struck. The man flinched, hand to shoulder, then sagged to one knee as the blotfish poison bit. Jaw locked. Breath sawed.

Jed was already moving. He slung the bow, dropped to the alley, and dragged the twitching weight into deep shadow behind a rain barrel before anyone could glance out the tavern door. For a heartbeat he hesitated. This one hadn't burned the warrens. This one hadn't smiled over Yarra's scream or Kep's vanished cry. His hand trembled on the knife hilt. The memory of his boy's weight filled his arms again—then empty, always empty. He set his teeth.

Two inches left of the carotid. In. Push. Twist. Out. The thrashing stilled; the alley went quiet.

Message.

Jed knelt. With a careful claw he carved his clan's jagged mark into the brow—lines clean and fast, the symbol his people had carried into every tunnel war. No human would mistake it.

He rifled the belt. Fingers closed on a small iron disk, stamped with the fanged wolf of the Blackenguard—proof of belonging, loyalty bought in coin. He slid it into his cloak pocket.

He scaled the wall again and vanished onto the rooftops.

The city stretched before him, its alleys breathing smoke and silence. Jed angled away from the tavern, running lightly across tile and beam until he reached a side street near another hall—this one belonging to a rival mercenary band. Their sign, a hammer crossed with chain, was painted above the door. A drunk nearby muttered to no one, "Not another guild war. Gods help us."

Jed crouched, pulled the wolf-head disk from his pocket, and let it fall. It clinked once on stone, spun, and came to rest near the threshold.

Let the wolves and the hounds tear at each other while he watched.

He slipped back toward the dockside alleys. Three turns and a low run along the quay's underside brought him to Brann's shack. The place was dark, the smell of fish stew still faint in the air. He set the crossbow on the table, pulled off the cloak, and sat in the silence. His ribs ached, his arms shook, but there was a calm beneath it.

And guilt. Guilt that he had brought this shadow to the only two souls who had given him bread and bandages instead of betrayal.

The game had begun. Now he would wait, listen, and set the next mark.

Chapter 17

Chapter Seventeen — The Squall

Rain battered the shack like fists on a hull. The alley ran like a crooked stream, gutters coughing salt and soot, and the roof shivered whenever the wind clawed it. Inside, the oil lamp hissed, throwing a shaky glow across crates, rope, and the scarred table.

Brann lounged with his boots on the table, tankard in one hand, stew slicking his beard. Jed sat near the stove, honing a bolt in slow, steady strokes. Each scrape cut through the storm. His ribs flared with every motion—iron bands reminding him how close he'd come to breaking.

"Word's out," Brann said at last, voice thick with ale. "They found the one you stuck. Right where you left him, though half the Watch swore he'd been dragged. Dockside's buzzing like a kicked hive. Whole city's chewing on it."

Jed kept scraping.

Brann leaned forward, voice dropping. "They say he was carved. Deep. A mark on his head—curse, gang sign, depends who's telling it. None of 'em know what it means. And wouldn't you know, a token turns up outside the Ivory Kraken's hall. Now the Blackenguard are foaming, pointing at the Krakens. Near came to blows in the square this morning." He barked a laugh. "If they gut each other, you'll be drinking victory without lifting a claw."

Jed glanced up, pale eyes flat. "Good."

Brann's brows rose. "Good?"

"They're fighting each other, not me," Jed said. "That was the point. Fear. Confusion. Let them draw the wrong blades."

Brann chuckled, unease threading the sound. "Sharp, I'll give you that. But carving that mark—that's a line, scales. Gets blood hot. Folk here—" he tapped the table "—folk remember rites and curses. Makes the Watch sniff harder."

Jed slid the bolt into its quiver. "They already hunt me. Better they chase ghosts than truth. And if my clan's name lives again, even once, it's worth it."

Brann shook his head, grinning. "Colder than a gull's beak. Gods, you're turning into a proper bastard." He tipped his tankard. "City loves a monster. They're already calling you the Rat-Dragon. Daft name, but it sticks."

Jed's jaw tightened; a faint smile tugged anyway. "Then let them believe it."

The door banged open and the storm shoved Mara inside. Cloak soaked, hair plastered to her brow, she kicked the door shut. Wind shrieked in the crack like it meant to drag her back out.

"Squall," she muttered, yanking off the cloak. "One of those bastard storms that'll snap half the moorings by dawn. Docks'll look like a graveyard." She wrung her sleeves and eyed them both. "What's the mood in here? Looks like someone pissed in the stew."

"Toasting our little genius," Brann said, raising his cup.

"Genius?" Mara snorted, moving to the stove. "Luck dressed like arrogance. Bold, sure. But cutting a mark in a man's head? That's not clever. That's a noose you braided yourself."

Jed met her stare. "You told me to think ahead. I did. Gave them fear where they thought they had power. Confusion instead of certainty."

"You gave them reason to sharpen the hunt," Mara shot back. She stirred too hard; broth slopped over the rim. "And don't forget why they hired Veynar to smoke your people out to begin with: the high houses pay wolves to 'clean' what they call unsavory—kobolds, beggars, anyone who doesn't fit their ledgers—so they can sell the city an illusion of safety. Cheaper than fixing sewers and hunger. Easier to call it order."

Brann lifted both hands. "Easy, lass. Don't skin him yet. He's thinking sharper than before. And gods help me, I think he likes it."

Jed's claws tapped the table. "I was a shoemaker once."

That stopped them both.

Brann blinked, then laughed like he'd been punched. "Shoemaker? I thought you were born mean. All this time bent over leather like some old cobbler?" He slapped the table. "Survive this and you owe me a pair. Stitched proper. None of this dock trash."

Jed's smile returned, thin. "Full price. Shoemaker's code."

Brann roared. "He smiles! Mara, look at that—teeth and everything."

She rolled her eyes, mouth twitching. "Two idiots haggling boots while the Watch sniff alleys. Truly, I'm cursed."

The curse turned to prophecy when the door shuddered under a heavy fist.

"City Watch!" a voice bellowed. "Open for inspection!"

Jed froze, ribs stabbing as he slid under the table—nothing but a flipped crate with boards nailed on. The dark stank of tar and wet rope. His heart hammered against bruises that flared like fire.

Brann started for the door, but Mara shouldered past, smoothing her hair and pasting on a smile before swinging it open. Rain and a cloaked sergeant came in together.

"Sergeant," Mara cooed. "Get in before the storm drowns you."

Water dripped off steel. The man's eyes flicked to Brann—narrowing—then back as Mara pressed a steaming bowl into his hands. "Warm yourself," she said lightly.

Brann scowled for show, playing the brute. Mara leaned on his arm, smile quick and knife-sharp. "Pay no mind to him. Just a sailor keeping me company on a storm night."

Brann flushed, catching the play. "Rough docks," he muttered. "Man's gotta keep the lady safe."

The sergeant slurped, gaze drifting. It landed on the crossbow propped against the wall—careless, damning.

Jed swore under his breath, claws biting grooves in the crate's belly.

"That yours?" the guard asked.

"Mine," Brann said without blinking. "Dockside's no place to walk barehanded."

Mara laughed, just a hair too quick. "Don't mind him. Couldn't hit the sea from the pier. His best weapon's a ladle."

The guard grunted, finished the bowl, and set it down. "Stay inside. Talk of a kobold—cut down a Blackenguard, carved him like a hog. People are calling it the Rat-Dragon. Fool name, but fools believe easy. Orders are to scour the alleys till we find it."

Jed's heart thundered. His claws split wood.

The sergeant tugged his cloak, nodded, and stepped back into the rain.

They listened to the footsteps fade. The storm hammered harder.

Brann exhaled. "Close as a razor's edge."

Mara rubbed her face, shoulders sagging. "If they're knocking in this weather, they'll be gutting alleys by morning."

Jed eased out, ribs flaring as he straightened. Furious with himself for leaving the crossbow out, he looked from one to the other, voice low but steady. "Then we sharpen."

In the lamp's unsteady glow, his pale eyes held something new. Not only grief—purpose.

Chapter 18

Waiting

The squall limped into morning as more rain than rage. The worst had passed, but Grayhaven still drowned under it. The docks were empty save for ropes creaking on sodden posts and the stray lantern bobbing in the mist. No fishmongers shouting, no sailors shouldering barrels—only rain hissing and wood groaning. Even Mara had shuttered her shop, muttering that the streets were too foul for trade and the damp would rot her herbs before anyone bought them. She'd gone back to her rooms to dry stock.

Brann had stumbled in near dawn, water sheeting from his cloak, boots squelching. He'd gone out after the watchman's visit—"Gossip doesn't wait for clear skies," he'd said—and returned with a brief report before collapsing into the side room, snoring like a sawmill.

"Best you don't prowl, scaly. Not safe. Mercs are moving in packs now—Blackenguard thick as weeds after rain. Krakens and Blackenguard brawled; half a tavern smashed. Then Veynar strolls in with that wolf-hide grin and has a quiet word with the Kraken lead. Fight vanishes like smoke. Word is he 'knows exactly' who killed his men. Didn't name you, but they're bristling like porcupines."

Now Jed sat alone on the floor in the main room. The storm worried the shutters and wormed chill into the wood. He'd spent the night stitching leather—Brann's new shoes—soles neat, seams tight, work that belonged to his old hands instead of the ones that killed. They sat on the table, finished, and he wondered whether craft meant anything at all.

Restlessness crawled his skin. The Watch sniffed for a Rat-Dragon. Mercenaries prowled in packs. Each night here set Mara and Brann closer to risk they hadn't asked to shoulder.

He shivered. The damp was in the walls and in his bones. He went to the stove, dug the tinder box, and cursed. Everything was wet—splinters dark with mold, cordwood soaked clean through. He stacked it anyway; it refused to catch.

He turned to hunt a blanket and walked face first into Brann's midsection.

Jed jerked back, swearing under his breath. Brann rubbed his eyes with a wet knuckle, sleep-drunk and grinning.

"Should've figured you'd get cold. Lizards like the sun, don't they?"

"I'm not a lizard, Brann."

Ignoring the bite, Brann shouldered him aside, hefted a sodden log, frowned, and rummaged in the cabinet. He came up with a squat bottle. The reek slapped Jed's nose—sharp enough to sting the eyes.

Brann sluiced a glug over the log, slicking the bark, shoved it into the stove, struck flint. Flame leapt—too fast, too bright—caught, roared, then settled to a steady burn, licking rain as if it weren't there.

Jed stared. "How did you—"

"Blackgut brew." Brann's grin widened. "Worse than piss to drink, but it'll set a river on fire. A mate tried passing it as rum once. Nearly killed the first man who swallowed. I keep it for this."

Jed watched the flame cling where no flame should. His claws flexed on his knees. A thought slid in—thin and sharp.

If a soaked log burned like that... what about a tarred beam?

He said nothing. The fire popped; the storm rattled the shutters. Brann rambled—sailors who'd drink anything for a kick, nights when gut-whiskey wasn't enough—but Jed only half heard. He was seeing a hall: the Blackenguard's beams, tar-fat and weather-swollen; men laughing over dice. A single spark. A rush of fire before they found their feet.

His tail twitched. His heart thumped slow and heavy.

Finally, low: "Brann... how much of that brew do you have?"

Brann froze mid-story, grin fading. He leaned back, weighing Jed like weather. "If you're set on dying, there are easier ways. Rope's quicker. Cleaner." A beard scratch. "But if you're serious—my mate left a stack when no one would buy. Three, maybe four crates in the warehouse. Can't rent the space; stinks too sharp. Why?"

Jed didn't answer. A coal dropped and hissed. Outside, rain drummed like fists.

He curled his claws into his cloak's hem. The thought burned now, dangerous and bright. He whispered, almost to himself:

"Because maybe this ends with fire."

Chapter 19

The Fire to Come

The next day the rain broke, leaving Grayhaven slick and steaming. The gutters ran black with pitch and ash, the boards of the docks swollen until nails moaned in their seams. The air clung heavy, sour with wet rope and fish guts turned rank. Every gull in the city seemed to have found its voice again, shrieking and fighting over scraps the storm had shaken loose.

Jed crouched by the crate they'd turned into a table, map unrolled on its battered lid. His claws traced the damp ink marks, but his eyes kept flicking toward the shadow at the quay—the wreck of a mast, broken in the storm, its lines trailing like severed veins. He thought of his own clan's mark-stone cracked in half, and how the tide had not cared.

Mara arrived with her usual storm of words. She always started with Brann. She cuffed him across the shoulder for some foolish thing he had said or done—and he took it with his sheepish grin, rubbing at the spot as if her hand were a blessing instead of a rebuke. Then her tongue turned sharp as fishbone at Jed, slicing across his silence with the ease of ritual.

"Fools, the both of you," she muttered, voice carrying above the gulls. "Can't leave you two alone without expecting to find you drowned, stabbed, or drunk under a table." She jabbed a finger at Jed's chest. "You especially. I swear, one day I'll find your corpse and it'll be grinning at me for the trouble."

Jed let her words wash over him. By now it was as much a rhythm as the tide—Mara's scolding, Brann's smirk, his own stillness. Sometimes he even caught himself smiling at her barbs, the way he used to smile when Yarra nagged him about the thread clinging to his scales.

Yarra.

The smile faltered, as if smoke had slipped through his chest. He bent lower over the map.

"All right, then," Mara said at last, planting her fists on her hips. "Brann's been nattering that you needed me. What's so important it couldn't wait for sense to find you?"

Jed tapped the map, claws clicking. "Here. The Blackenguard guildhall. Brann says the mercenaries are cautious now—they travel in groups, they come back together before curfew. My guess is Veynar ordered it himself."

"Hold." Mara's voice snapped sharp enough to cut through gulls and waves alike. She leaned in, eyes narrowing. "If you're planning on marching straight into their den, I'll box your ears right here and stab you myself. Save me the trouble of sewing you back together afterward."

Brann barked a laugh. "She means it too. I've seen her stitch a man's lip shut while he was still talking."

Mara's glare silenced him, but only for a breath.

Jed drew a steady line with his claw across the map. "I'm not the same kobold you had to sew back together, Mara. The storm's lightened the Watch's patrols. The mercs huddle inside that hall every night. One roof, one fire, and they'll all roast in their own den."

Mara raised a brow, unimpressed. "Turn the guildhall into an oven, is that it? Clever words, but words don't burn timbers. And you think you're the first fool I've patched up after a blaze? I've seen men burned to bone, screaming for mothers who couldn't hear. I've seen council brats slip to my door at night with their skin split from brawls, coin in hand to keep me quiet. Knives, poison, bruises—the city hides those. Fire?" She shook her head. "Fire's a beacon. It draws eyes money can't smother."

Jed lifted his snout, a glint of satisfaction in his eyes. "I've thought it through."

Brann laughed again, slapping his knee. "Look at him, pleased as a gull with a fish head. You can teach an old rat new tricks."

"Dog," Mara corrected. "And don't flatter him yet." She leaned closer, jabbing at the map again. "Two problems. One, you have to get close enough to light it. Two, after three days of storm, those timbers are wetter than a sailor's promises. You'll get smoke, not fire."

Brann's grin only widened. From beneath the crate, he dragged up a bottle, the glass dark and sticky at the lip. He thumped it down between them like a prize. "That's where I come in."

Jed eyed it. Blackgut. The reek of it stung even from behind the cork, thick as tar.

Mara gave the bottle one glance, then another at Brann, who was positively glowing with smugness. "This is your plan? You mean to drown a building in swill? Be easier to pour it down their throats and let them poison themselves."

Jed opened his mouth, but Mara cut him off with a raised hand. "Don't speak. It's not a bad plan, Jed, I'll give you that. Crafty, even. But don't forget—I still hear secrets no physician should. Half this city limps through my shop when they can't pay the guild doctors, or when they need a quiet hand that won't tell tales. I know which councilors pay the Watch to look away. I know which mercs leave their blood on my table. Fire changes that balance. Burn a hall, and every man with coin and cause will want a throat for the gallows. Likely yours."

Jed's claws curled against the crate, dragging faint lines through the damp wood. "I know." His voice was low, steady as stone. "But this needs to end. They came to my warren. I will go to theirs."

The words sat heavy between them. Brann shifted, his grin faltering, while Mara drummed her fingers against the crate in that quick, staccato rhythm she always fell into when she was thinking. Tap-tap-tap, faster than her tongue, sharp as rain on a ship's deck.

She glanced sideways at Brann. "The SilverFish crew still in port?"

Brann scratched his chin. "Rowdy lot. But I got them to mind their manners last I saw."

97

Mara's mouth curled, half a smile, half a blade. "This time I'll need them not to mind their manners. When are they shipping out?"

Jed blinked. He followed their words like a man following the tide's pull—he did not understand every current, but he felt the weight of it. Dockside names still tangled in his head like knots. He knew only that Brann always seemed to know who was in port, which captains swaggered, which owed coin.

"Their mast took a beating in the storm," Brann said after a moment. "Won't be sailing for a week at least."

"Good." Mara tapped the bottle of blackgut once with her nail, thoughtful. "Their captain owes me a favor from last time he was here. He'll remember. I'll make sure of it."

Jed didn't ask what sort of favor. With Mara, there was always a story—and a debt.

She looked back at him, the sharpness in her face easing just a fraction. "All right, little rat. We'll get your walls painted in this filth. Might take a few days, but it'll be done. Till then, stay out of trouble."

Jed gave a short, humorless snort. "What kind of trouble can I get into? I'm locked up with Brann for company. My roommate snores."

Brann narrowed his eyes at him, then swung to Mara. "See? Told you. He's been cracking more and more jokes lately. Bad ones, but jokes. Must be catching it from me."

Mara barked a laugh, sudden and sharp. "Gods help us all if that's true."

Jed almost smiled again—almost—before the memory of Yarra's voice pulled it back down. He lowered his gaze to the map. The ink had bled in the rain, but the lines still led to the guildhall. One roof. One fire.

And one name that still needed cutting into the dark.

Chapter 20

Fire in the Night

The next days dragged like a net across rock.

Jed tried to make time move by carving it into tasks. He counted bolts—twenty—laying each one out on Brann's crate until the heads sat like a row of teeth. He checked the crossbow twice, then again: string waxed, nut clean, stirrup tight, stock oiled with fish grease because that was what he had. He stitched scraps to quiet the creak of leather when he moved. He sharpened his knife, set it aside, then sharpened it again—knowing he wouldn't use it tonight, knowing equally well that hands without work start clawing at a body from the inside.

Cabin fever, Brann called it. Jed called it pacing until the boards learned his footfall and creaked at the right spots.

When his head was too loud he made things small again. He cut soft-soled shoes for Mara to match the ones he'd made for Brann—leather thin and quiet, stitching tight enough no water would creep. He worked the awl as if each hole were a breath he could control: in, press, twist, out. The rhythm helped until it didn't, and then he sat in the dark, listening to the shack sweat and the harbor breathe.

Mara had said to wait, so he waited.

Brann passed gossip and told how the Rat-Dragon's excitement was embering into a story. Good. Quiet makes a bigger bang.

Mara's plan was simple the way knives are simple. The SilverFish crew—born to the art of stumbling, gleeful at the science of getting away with it—would stagger past the Blackenguard guildhall loud enough to wake the gulls. Bottles would fly. Watchmen would watch. The south wall would wear a coat of blackgut, and no one would ask why the whole street stank like a ship's heart. Jed would do the rest.

He'd almost worn a groove in Brann's floorboards when the door slammed open hard enough to rattle the windows.

Jed's body moved before his thoughts. He went low, knife up, every muscle wanting to be elsewhere.

"It's done," Brann gasped, bent double, red-faced from the run. He waved a hand, panting. "Gods damn—the Watch took it too far. One of the guards stabbed Liam in the belly. Had to swarm in after that. But the south wall—by the door—" He grinned, all teeth and sweat. "Painted in blackgut. Whole street smells to high hell. Everyone shrugs it off as 'sailors brawling.'"

Jed felt his claws ease out of his palms.

"Mostly pride and fat lost," Brann added quickly. "Mara's with him. You know how she gets."

Jed did. He nodded once. The nod felt like a blade turning. The hook had set. Now the line would pull.

He waited for night because Mara had told him to wait, and because he had promised Yarra somewhere under his breath that he would learn patience or die trying. The waiting turned his bones to wire. He made himself eat—four mouthfuls of stale bread dipped in fish oil—because a body without salt shakes at the wrong time. He sat with his back against the wall and breathed the way they had sung in the warrens: low and even, the short songs meant to keep breath steady in tight places.

When the city exhaled and its lamps burned thin, he went.

He wrapped himself in the quiet cloak, sling and knife left under the sleeping shelf as if he'd molted. The crossbow rode his spine; the quiver hugged his ribs. He checked the fire striker twice, then once more, because superstition is just another word for the prayers your hands make. He tied Yarra's red thread tight around his wrist until it ached.

Brann caught his forearm as he slipped past. "Don't stay to count," he said, eyes uncharacteristically sober. "Shoot and go."

Jed bared his teeth. "I'm small. I know the math."

Brann still didn't let go. "Mara said I should tell you to run if anything goes wrong." He snorted. "She also said you won't."

"Tell Mara I listened," Jed said, and pulled free.

The rooftops remembered him. Slate to beam to rope: the city's higher roads under his feet again. The damp made everything mean and slick. He moved when the wind moved, when gulls cried, when a door slammed below—he ghosted along the noises the city made without him and became one more. Between houses, the harbor opened: a black plate scored by lanterns, the piers jutting like broken ribs. Bells somewhere—not alarm yet, just time being scratched into the night.

He went past the Broken Net, past the ropewalk where tar seams bled black and sweet, past the warehouse they'd burned before, now a husk. Men had chalked his sigil on its stones since, crude copies. Children had smudged them with dirty fingers. He did not look long.

The Blackenguard guildhall hunched where the quay stepped back from the river's bite. Stone lower walls, timber upper; windows narrow enough to be mean. A lantern hung over the door like a tongue. The south wall—the one facing the river and the alley that funneled any wind straight along it—glistened in a way wood doesn't. Even from above he could smell it: blackgut, thick and sour, the stink that lives under decks and makes lantern-light crawl.

He belly-crawled to the lip of the roof opposite and lay there, small in the shadow line, chin just above the parapet.

Inside the hall, light still moved—lanterns passing from table to table, men cursing softly. He counted them without trying. Bodies make different shadows than chairs. Boots make different sounds from benches. He listened with the part of himself that had learned to measure leather with fingers and weigh rope with his palm. When the lights began to go—one by one, steady, not alarmed—his body eased into the angle he needed.

He set the crossbow between his knees, hands slow and sure. He drew a bolt—the one he'd prepped last night: head wrapped with rag, rag soaked and dried and soaked again in blackgut until it would take a spark the way a story takes a crowd.

The first flare, if you're not a fool, you make with your body blocking the wind.

He cupped his hands around the rag and struck flint to steel. A soft spit of light—another—then a lace of flame took, trembled, licked his knuckles. He could smell his own scales singe. He breathed out through his teeth and fed it another breath. It grew hungry, began to eat.

He brought the bow up, the burning bolt blurring his night eye, and settled the stock to his shoulder the way he'd practiced until the bruises against his collarbone had turned to a small, hard comfort. He took the south wall into his sights—the part above the door where the wind would love the flame best, where the blackgut would hold it up and whisper yes.

"Wait for the breath," Yarra had once said in some other life, when he'd tried to start a coal with too much impatience and too proud a lung. "Not a blow. A breath."

He breathed. He loosed.

The bolt hissed across. For a heartbeat it was a star; then it struck. The rag kissed the wall and spread itself like a smile. The fire took in an instant—too eager, too bright, as if it had been waiting for permission. It crawled, then sprinted, the blackgut beneath becoming a fuse that ran both ways at once, up and down, left and right, hungry and sure.

For a terrible pause, nothing else. Flame can show off before it does the work. Jed waited through that silence—had they scraped it off, had rain made a liar of him—and then the pitch in the seams joined. Light leapt like a dropped lantern. The night went orange.

Shouts inside. A chair went over. Boots thumped. Someone cursed Veynar by name. Someone else laughed—a hysteric sound—right before the laugh became a scream.

Jed ducked low, shrinking to the rooftop, and cranked the bow. The string came back smooth; the nut caught. He slid the next bolt in—plain iron, no flame—and sighted on the door. Flames licked the jambs now. Smoke groped at the lintel.

The first mercenary in the doorway had his cloak up over his mouth and no helmet. His eyes were wrong with panic. Jed shot him through the chest where the cloak edge made a target. The man pinwheeled backward into the heat with a sound that's the same in every language.

Jed did not count after that. He aimed when he could, loosed when he couldn't—every bolt part of a rhythm that blurred aim and instinct into one thing. Pull, set, breathe, send. Sometimes his sights found eyes or throats. Sometimes they only found panic. Precision became hunger. The doorway clogged with bodies that solved his problem.

Smoke blew out, then in. The night had a wind now; Jed felt it change along his cheek. Fire loved it.

Men on the upper story decided windows are doors if you are on fire. One smashed; a man came out not like a man but like a torch that knew how to scream. He hit the cobbles and rolled because training stays even inside panic. The oil made rolling worse. Jed had spent his mercy already for the evening and looked away.

His quiver grew light. The orange changed to a whiter thing as structural timber learned what heat meant. Flame bellowed like a throat too full, then drew a huge breath and exhaled. Inside, the big beams gave that particular sound—like a ship deciding to turn on its crew.

Bells now. Real ones, the Watch's brass throats opening. A shout across rooftops: "To! To!" Buckets somewhere. Boots.

Jed loosed until the rhythm stopped needing thought. When the last bolt left his bow, the hall was already an oven and the fire sang victory in crack and roar.

The bow clicked empty. He set it down by feel and rolled sideways along the roof's belly. Across the way, the guildhall lurched, a drunk pinned upright only by its own timbers. Then the spine of it sighed—as if exhausted by holding the world up for men who didn't deserve it—and folded in on itself. A billow of sparks leapt into the air and scattered like a flock of birds changing its mind.

"Rooftops!" a voice below—not a prayer, a Watchman's curse. "Rooftops!"

Jed was already moving. He slid into the trough of dark between chimneys and lashed himself forward along the path he'd traced in his head for three days. A coil of rope he'd hidden under a loose tile came up smooth; he looped it over the gable's tooth and swung the gap to the next roof with a quick, mean grace that would have made him sick with pride if he'd had a second to feel it.

The Watch knew the streets. They did not know the slates like a kobold who learned balance in tunnels too narrow to forgive mistakes. He moved like shadow across the tiles, but shadows don't stop dogs from sniffing or men from stumbling close. Skill carried him most of the way; luck carried him the rest. Tonight, both were thin.

A dog below sniffed at hot air and whined. Jed flattened against the parapet and became stone. The dog pulled; the handler swore; the crowd shoved back to watch the burn, because people are always the same when fire is free: they want to see. That crush saved him better than any spell.

He cut down into the alley three houses over, where a rope already hung from a wedge under a gutter with a knot at just the right height for his hands. He went down it silent, knees light as gulls, and took two steps into the shadow his body had measured at noon when he'd watched the sun find corners. A Watchman clattered up the stair opposite with his cudgel out and his chest up, brave as bread. Jed waited until the man's own noise drowned him, then slid sideways through a door jimmied last winter and never fixed, into a courtyard strung with wet laundry and the smell of cheap soap.

He left the crossbow under a rain barrel in a corner he'd selected—wrapped, a stone wedged to make it look like trash—and angled his small body through a gap where a fence had rotted.

A boy and a cat stared at him from under a stair.

Jed froze. His body, still wired for kill-and-move, almost lifted the knife out of instinct—loose ends are danger. The mercs had taught him that tonight: hesitation stacked bodies in doorways. For a half-breath the blade wanted to leap.

But the boy did not move. He only watched, eyes wide, steady as if he'd been carved from the same stone Jed had become on the rooftops. Eyes too big for his face. Eyes that belonged to another boy.

Kep.

Jed's grip went slack. He slid the knife back against his ribs as if it had burned him. He bared his teeth in what might have been a smile and put a finger to his snout. The boy did not nod. He simply held his cat closer and kept watching, silent as any witness.

Jed pulled himself through the fence gap without another sound, but his chest ached worse than the bruised ribs ever had.

The bells receded behind him and then swung back again as more men took up the call. The city ran toward the fire in some places and away in others. Jed moved perpendicular to both.

By the time he reached the edge of the docks, the light behind him made the harbor shine unnatural and the smoke had been shouldered inland by the sea breeze. He took the long way along the wetter boards, where footprints blur and noses give up. The gulls had gone quiet. Even birds know when heat is too much for air.

He did not stop moving until the water's sound cut everything else.

Chapter 21

The Rope Still Hung

The shack smelled of wet salt and old rope, but to Jed it had come to smell of reprieve. Outside, the storm had finally broken. Sun steamed the dock planks until gulls wheeled loud in the clear air, fighting over scraps shaken loose by the night's violence. Inside, it was quieter—just the creak of drying timbers and Brann's boots by the door, mud flaking from their seams.

Jed sat cross-legged by the crate that served as their table, one claw working a strip of leather. For the first time in months, he felt lighter. Something long-knotted in his chest had loosened enough that he could bend to his work without every heartbeat screaming. His clan, his family—Yarra, Kep—their debt had been answered. The hall had burned. For once, they burned.

Soon, he told himself, he would say goodbye to this shack. To Brann with his loud laugh and easy shoulders. To Mara with her sharp tongue and a needle like judgment. Not just friends—family of another kind. They had taken him in when he crawled half-dead from the docks. For a time, Grayhaven itself had been a hiding place.

But that hiding was done. The Watch would be relentless now. He could not stay—not after the guildhall's ashes. He would leave the city before dawn, vanish into roads he had not walked in years. The thought made his tail tap once, a soft punctuation against the boards. Leaving would hurt, but he had carried worse.

He was still turning over how to tell them—how to put words around gratitude without softening his scales—when the door slammed open.

Mara filled the threshold, hair damp with mist, shoulders squared as if she had braced herself before stepping in. Brann stumbled behind her, breathless, red-faced from running.

"Woman, I said to wait!" he barked, grabbing at her arm. "Let me—"

"Jed," Mara cut him off, voice low, flat, too controlled. Her eyes fixed on him like knives set to a whetstone. "Veynar was not in the building. Not last night."

The strip of leather slipped from Jed's claws.

Brann swore. "Damn it, woman, I told you to wait. You're supposed to be the one with brains."

Jed's ears tilted forward, slow, unbelieving. "What?"

Brann swallowed, then said it anyway. "What Mara says is true. Heard it from one of the bastards myself. Turns out Veynar wasn't there. Been staying at another house across the city."

Jed's heart lurched. Relief turned to ruin in a breath. All the fragile loosening, the sense of debt repaid—it slammed back down like a roof collapsing. Smoke filled his lungs again. Yarra's mouth opened to speak and never did. Kep's small breath cut short. The rope of Veynar's smile, uncut, still hung.

Brann saw it hit him and forced him into the chair by the crate. "Now listen. You ruined his guild. You made your point. Way I see it, you're even. That's it. That's enough."

Mara shook her head. Her voice sharpened, and beneath it trembled something Jed had never heard from her—fear. "Both of you, listen. I didn't tell you so you could go running after him. I told you because you need to leave with your scales still on your hide. That man is unhinged. He'll stop at nothing now. It won't take long to piece it together—the sailors' brawl, the blackgut fire. It all points one way." She softened, and it chilled Jed more than her anger ever had. "Jed, you have to go."

But Jed's mind was already racing. No. It wasn't finished. He could not leave a rope hanging. He dragged the map across the crate's scarred surface. "Where is this safe house?"

"Jed—" Mara began, but the word tore.

"We cannot help you any further than this," she said, softer than he had ever heard her—softer than knives, softer than judgment. It was a voice she must have used once for someone she loved, spent now on him, begging him back from the fire.

Brann set a hand on her shoulder, steadying her. His own eyes were wet at the corners though he would not admit it. "Scales, we messed up. I should've found out sooner. Now we're all in danger. Mara's right—won't be long till Veynar puts two and two together, and then he'll be here. It's time to abandon ship."

A knock at the door froze them. Brann went to answer, muttering curses.

He came back with a folded scrap clenched in his fist. The paper was damp, corners smudged as if the runner hadn't dared linger in the open.

He handed it to Jed without a word.

Jed opened it. Not words. A drawing. Quick lines, practiced: the outline of a street, a corner, a single building marked like prey on a hunter's map. He recognized it at once. He had passed it a hundred times on the north side, never sparing it a thought. Now it was a wolf's den.

"This is where he's staying," Brann said grimly. His mouth twisted as if the words tasted bad. "Jed, I'm leaving in two days with the SilverFish. We're taking her up the coast for a while. Mara's coming, too. You've got two days until we sail."

Two days. A clock struck into his bones. Two days to leave with them—or to finish what fire had not.

Jed's claws pressed into the paper until it tore.

The rope still hung.

Chapter 22

The Decision

Brann and Mara left him with the smell of salt rope and the silence of their absence. The door settled soft, but Jed felt it like a slammed gate. He could still see their faces—Brann's jaw tight with the words he wanted to force down Jed's throat; Mara's eyes sharp with fear and, worse beneath it, care.

He could still see the runner's face, too. The knock had come moments earlier, quick as a gull's peck. Brann had cracked the door on its chain and grunted, then let the boy slip inside out of the drizzle. Dock-runner: bare feet, ribs like a tally, a red thread of old blood at the hairline. Brann trusted him—"Kerr," he'd said, tossing a copper to the boy's quick hand, "fastest legs on the quay." Jed knew him before the name landed. Same eyes as the alley—wide, steady, clutching a crust to his chest while three men closed in. The boy saw Jed, froze a heartbeat, then set his jaw as if to say he remembered and would not speak it. He pressed a folded scrap into Brann's palm and vanished back into the weather the way small things do when the world is hunting larger prey. Brann handed the note to Jed: a narrow map, a street and a single house marked like prey.

Jed sat on the floor with that crude map spread across the crate like an accusation. Claws traced lines, the corner, the marked house. A wolf's den sketched by a nervous hand.

He lay back and watched the dark beams overhead. Let the thoughts come. Smoke. Screams. The hall cracking in fire. Men coughing their last. Dogs baying. Veynar's fists. His own ribs breaking. He flinched once—even in memory.

Other faces pushed through. Brann's wide, foolish grin over dice. Mara's scolding tongue hiding the way she slid bread across when she thought he hadn't eaten enough. They had never spat vermin at him. Never asked him to be anything but what he was.

For a heartbeat he rested there—Yarra's gentle chiding when his stitches ran crooked, Kep's small heel in his palm, Yarra's brow bumping his in the old way.

Then it broke. The laughter stopped. The roof fell. Kep's breath cut short under stone. Yarra's scream swallowed by smoke. A wolf-pelt filling the tunnel light. Veynar's smile.

Jed sat so fast the room lurched. He snatched the map. His claws trembled and tore the parchment before he knew he meant to. The rip sounded like a bone-snap. He stared at the ragged edge, breath rasping, and felt something in him tear with it.

No calm. No patience. The rope would not hang.

He shoved the map aside and reached for Mara's knife. The blade gleamed too clean for what it was meant for. The crossbow was gone; that didn't matter. Fire had done its work on wood. This would be work for his hands.

The shack had turned too small, the air sour and briny, walls pressing. Brann's boots by the door, the leather strip he'd been stitching—nothing mattered. He pushed to his feet, tail lashing once, and slid the knife into his belt. He bound Yarra's red thread around his wrist until it hurt.

Tonight, scout. Tomorrow, cut.

He yanked the door. The hinge squealed like a rat. He stepped into Greyhaven's wet dark.

Streets gleamed—slick black under a low belly of cloud. Lanterns along the quay guttered, swinging blades of light across puddles and into alleys before drowning in shadow. The city breathed heavy, storm on its tongue. Jed pulled his hood low, slid into that breath, and moved.

He kept to gutters and rooflines, claws testing slate, tail low for balance. Noise was death. Steps timed to a watchman's cough, a loose shutter's slap, rain hissing on hot tar. He followed the crude lines he'd memorized, corner by corner, until the north quarter closed around him—houses shouldering tight, vinegar and tallow in the air. The marked house sat where the map had promised: pressed between a cooper's and a leaning storehouse, shutters closed, posture wary.

Two guards paced before the door. Red sashes at the arm. Swords at hip, pipes working. Not tavern swagger—men expecting trouble and wanting to meet it half a step early. Ten paces apart. Pause. Switch. Ten paces back. Jed hummed the count until the rhythm settled in his bones.

Higher.

He slid into the alley's shadow, climbed where mortar remembered old ladders, and flattened along the roofline. Slate slick, but this was his craft. Holds other feet had forgotten. A low lip where rain paused before deciding where to go. He made himself small above the house and looked down.

There—a skylight breaking the roofline. Iron bars thick as thumbs. Rust along the welds like a scab, but the set was deep. Not a slip-through. Not with tools he didn't have. Not with guards at the door and a storm building its own drum.

Lamplight pushed faint through shutter cracks. Once, something broad crossed that glow—shoulders, the rise of fur where light caught a pelt. A shadow, gone. Jed's claws dug crescents into slate.

Not yet. Not like this.

He slid back an arm's length, letting the pitch hide him from the street, and watched. The guards' turns. The pipe ember brightening on the pause. A slight dip in the roof where water pooled, three handspans left of the skylight. Acid and time would need a rope to marry both. Fire hot enough to eat iron would need a chimney's throat or the right wind. He counted gutters, weighed angles, measured rain.

Twice the Watch went by—dogs straining, harness jingling like teeth. Jed went still and thin as slate. The dogs lifted their heads at the storm's taste and whined rather than barked; handlers swore at reins tangling their own boots. When they passed, he breathed again through his nose, slow as tide.

113

He waited until the lamplight inside thinned and tired. The guards' pattern softened there—pipes shorter, the pause longer, one man rolling a shoulder the same way each turn. He stacked it all neat in his head, a cobbler's pile: this crack, this count, this hinge slow, this rail slick.

He traced his clan mark once with a claw-tip on the slate and let the wind erase it.

Enough for tonight.

The climb down was slower—every slate a lie waiting to slide. A gull swept low hoping for spillage, saw only night, and cursed him for a fool in its own tongue. Jed ghosted the gutter, slipped a handhold where rain had rotted wood, and found the alley again, small and sure. A watchman clattered past at the mouth with his chest up, brave as bread; Jed bled into a doorway he'd jimmied last winter and never fixed. He came out into a court strung with laundry that never dried, soap sour in the damp. A cat and a boy watched from under the stair. He bared his teeth in what might have been a smile and put a finger to his snout. The boy didn't nod—only watched with eyes too wide, like Kep's the first time he'd seen the upper tunnels.

Jed swallowed the name before it escaped. He moved.

By the time the docks opened at the alleys' end, the air had gone heavy. The gulls were quiet. Out beyond the masts, the horizon pulsed with a smear of lightning. Another storm, shouldering itself together. Good. Storms make clumsy men and generous shadows.

He took the wetter boards where footprints blur and noses give up, listening for pursuit, hearing only Greyhaven turning in its sleep. He slipped into Brann's shack as the first drops hissed on the roof and shut the door with his back, breathing deep. The torn map still lay on the crate. He didn't touch it. He set Mara's knife beside it. Lightning found the steel, and it answered.

Outside, wind shook the shack until ropes in the rafters groaned. Jed sat with his hands tight on his knees and let the storm talk.

It would hide his second climb. It would hide everything but the choice.

114

Chapter 23

Storm at the Door

The storm pressed against the shack in waves. Rain pattered, then pelted, then hammered until the ropes in the rafters groaned. Jed hunched over the crate, the map damp beneath his claws. His eyes burned from a night without sleep. He tapped the mark he'd drawn again and again until the paper split.

Brann stirred, swinging his legs off the cot. Mara was already awake, mending a net by lamplight. Her hands moved too sharp for the work. Both of them watched him, waiting.

"I found it," Jed said—low, flat with exhaustion. "The house. Guards at the door. Two. Swords and sashes. They walk like men used to it. And a skylight above—iron-barred, rusted, but strong. Couldn't slip through."

Mara's hands stilled. Brann frowned, tugging at his beard.

Jed pressed on, each word dragged out of him, heavy as stone. "To cut through, I'll need acid. Nothing else will do."

The shack filled with rain-noise. Water beat the roof hard enough that Jed's ears tilted, judging if it would hold.

Brann leaned forward, elbows on knees, no bluster in him. "So that's it. You've made up your mind."

Jed met his gaze without flinching. "Veynar still breathes. As long as he does, the rope hangs. You've both risked enough already. If I walk away now, it all falls on you. This ends with him."

Mara's needle slipped. The thread snapped. She stood fast, the net dropping to the floor. "Ends with him?" The words shook with something deeper than anger. "Jed, look around. This is already ending. Brann and I are packing what little we have because of that fire you lit at the guildhall. The Watch will be on us by tomorrow. You think killing Veynar fixes that?"

Jed's claws dug into the map until the parchment creased and tore. "It fixes him."

Her laugh came bitter, sharp. "Fixes him? And what about you? What's left when you've carved your last mark? You think Yarra would want this? You think Kep would smile to see what his father's become?"

The heat under Jed's ribs flared, but he didn't break. "They're already gone. He isn't. That's the truth of it."

Mara's jaw trembled. She wrenched her eyes away, shoved past Brann, and yanked her cloak from the peg. Wind punched through the open door, spraying rain into the room. "Fine. You won't listen. You never do. I'll get your damned acid. But don't expect me here when you crawl back with blood on your claws."

The door slammed. Her footsteps vanished under the downpour.

Brann stayed where he was, rubbing his face, lines dug deep. At last he rose and set a heavy hand on Jed's shoulder. No grin, no jest—only weight.

"If you're going to do this, scales," he said quietly, "be careful. That's all I'll say."

He followed her into the rain, leaving Jed alone with the storm.

Time stretched. Nails of water drove against the roof. Thunder cracked close enough to rattle his ribs. Jed sat cross-legged, staring at the knife on the crate while the storm clawed at the shutters, hunting its way in. He tried to breathe the way they'd sung in the warrens—short songs for tight air. The room smelled of wet rope and boiled tar. It steadied him and made him sick in the same breath.

He stood because sitting turned his bones to wire. He moved through the space once, twice, hands making work where there wasn't any. He cut a length of Brann's tarred line to waist height and tied a harness knot by feel—left over right, bite the bight, dress the turn—because knots listen when people won't. He checked the leather satchel he'd carry tonight: cloth pads, waxed twine, a stoppered skin for rinse-water, a rag to wrap around his nose and mouth. If the acid steamed, he'd need a breath he could trust. He found beeswax in Brann's kit and thumbed it into the seams of a little clay cup so the stuff wouldn't dribble where it shouldn't. Work turned the hour.

Rain rattled harder. Shadows walked past the shutter—two men together. The latch ticked once as a wind-gust lifted it. Jed went still and thin, a habit more than a choice. Voices slogged by—Watch, by the rhythm and the cursing. One lantern paused, its light pressuring the cracks in the wood slats. Jed could smell their wet wool, the dog on the end of the line. The dog's paws scratched once at the threshold, then the handler yanked, and both moved on under the shout of thunder. The shack exhaled with him.

A knock, quick and nervous, tapped the door.

Jed's claws found the knife before thought did. He waited. The knock came again, three beats—one, one-two—the dock code Brann used for "ours."

He slid the latch, blade low. A boy stood there in the rain, hair plastered to his skull, a scar of old bruise fading along one cheek. He clutched a waxed packet to his chest like bread. The cat from under the stair would have known him; Jed did, too—the street-scrap from the alley long ago, the one who'd run because a stranger in a cloak had bought him a heartbeat.

"Brann's runner," the boy said, shivering. "He said give you this and don't wait for coin." His eyes flicked to Jed's face and stayed. They didn't widen this time. He knew what he was looking at. Maybe he'd always known.

Jed took the packet. Inside lay a coil of thin copper wire, a pair of small tongs, and a note scrawled in Brann's blunt hand: If you must melt iron, do it at the joints. Don't breathe the steam. Tie off twice.

"Thank you," Jed said. The words came out rough. He fumbled at his belt-pouch and found two coppers. The boy shook his head once, quick, stubborn.

"Brann said no coin," he repeated, as if that settled the world.

Jed tucked the coppers back. He bent without thinking and lifted a corner of the boy's sodden hood, checking the fading bruise with a thumb he

117

kept gentle. "Keep to the lee in a storm," he murmured in the boy's own language—dock-slang, not Draconic. "Streets eat small feet when the drains are full."

The boy's mouth tightened like he'd learned not to smile where men could see. "Aye," he said. His gaze dropped to the red thread on Jed's wrist, then back up to Jed's eyes. Something like understanding passed between them—thin as a hair, strong as a bowstring. He stepped back into the rain and vanished along the wall as if he'd been born out of it.

Jed sealed the door, set the wire and tongs on the crate, and read the notes twice more. He placed a little dish of ash beside the vials he didn't yet have. The room felt larger for having something he could actually hold against iron.

At last the door shoved open again. Mara slammed it behind her, cloak dripping, her face wet with more than rain. She dropped a wrapped bundle onto the crate. Glass clinked inside.

"There," she said. Her voice was raw. "Your acid. Do what you will."

She didn't look at him. But her hands were steady as she peeled the oilcloth back and set each piece where it belonged, the way a surgeon lays out knives. Three small vials, glass thick and greenish. A fourth bottle of vinegar. A palmful of fine ash in a folded paper. "Rag over your face," she said—still not meeting his eyes. "Don't pour. Drip. Joints only. If it runs, dam it with wax or cloth. Vinegar after. Ash last. And—" Her voice twitched. "And if the fumes bite, you step back. You hear me? You step back."

Jed nodded, once. "I hear."

She pushed the ash packet against his chest; he took it. Her thumb brushed the red thread at his wrist and stilled there for a heartbeat, as if testing whether the knot held. Then she pulled away like it had burned her.

The wind punched the shack again. Brann's shadow crossed the shutters and the door swung in. He stamped water off his boots and set a small iron hook on the table—a grapnel he'd cut down to a quiet size. "If you're dropping in a hole, might as well climb out of one," he said, trying for lightness and failing halfway. His eyes found the boy's wet footprints on the floorboards and softened, then went hard again on Jed. "You've got what you asked for. Now you've got to be smarter than the man you hate."

Jed tucked the hook with the wire and the vials. He wound Yarra's red thread tighter around his wrist until it bit scale.

The storm roared above.

There was only one path.

Chapter 24

The Storm Waits

The storm would not leave the shack alone. It pressed at the boards in bands and pulses—rain first a patter, then a hammering—wind shouldering the walls until rafters groaned like an old hull straining at sea. Ropes creaked on their pegs. A corner shutter beat itself raw against the frame until someone—the last someone left here—lashed it down with frayed cord. The air held wet salt and old smoke and the stale edge of lamp oil. There was no silence to be had, only different sizes of noise.

Jed sat cross-legged on the floor by the crate that served as a table, the crude map spread under his claws. He had traced the same lines so many times the ink had lifted, black rubbed to a charcoal smear: north quarter; that crooked lane with the vinegar stink; the square of a roof; a bar scratched across it because the glass was caged in iron. In the corner, he had drawn two tiny slashes side by side for the guards. He drew them again. And again. And again—until their rhythm lived in his hands.

The crossbow was long gone. His skiff was cinders. The rope still hung.

He laid the knife beside the map, handle toward his right, blade toward the shutter slit where lightning blinked. Mara's knife—plain, honest steel, the edge he had kept kinder than his days. He ran the sling cords through his fingers, feeling for fray in the wet. The stones he'd chosen waited in a shallow bowl: six smooth picks the size of plum pits, river-polished, dark as the street water the storm was raking down toward the sea.

On the cot, Brann lay on his side with his back to Jed, broad shoulders hunched, a blanket thrown over him that did nothing against the damp. He wasn't sleeping. He hadn't slipped all the way into sleep since yesterday, and certainly not since the map appeared. He lay like a man trying to hear a thing he didn't want through a wall he could not move.

Jed worked the rope next—dock line taken from the peg near the door, thirty feet of tired hemp with enough life left to hold him one more time. He re-coiled it so it would feed clean from his shoulder, then tested knots until motion was muscle and breath again. A bowline he could tie with his eyes shut. A clove to catch on a chimney and hold. A prusik loop he might or might not need if the climb turned bad and he had to inch instead of leap. He stripped an old rag and wrapped a sling of cloth to bind a vial against his palm if he needed both hands at once.

Thunder rolled. Brann shifted and groaned once into the blanket.

"Two days," Jed said, not looking up from the rope.

Brann's voice came out low and rasped, worn thin by a night of weather and the day before it. "One and a half, now."

"Enough," Jed said.

Brann sat up, blanket falling from him, heavy with wet. He rubbed at his face with both hands, then let them hang between his knees. He looked older in storms, as if rain had weight years didn't. "You set on it."

"Yes." Jed kept his hands moving. If he stopped, the storm would fill the room with its own arguments. "I scouted. Two guards. The window's caged. The skylight is the only way that gets me where I need to be. I'll use the roofs. The thunder will cover me."

"The storm will tear you off them," Brann said. There was no laughter in him. The man who usually found a joke in a spilled barrel or a cracked tooth had gone quiet, hollowed to plain words.

"Then I fall," Jed said. "Or I don't."

Brann huffed through his nose. "Scales."

Jed finished wrapping the rag-loop, cinched it, and breathed once through the brine-thick air. He held up the knife and watched lightning skitter across the steel in miniature. "If I don't go, he'll come. He'll come here. To you."

"We'll be gone." Brann's eyes flicked to the corner where a short sea-bag sat open. He hadn't packed much. Dockside people didn't own much to begin with, and storm seasons taught you to count only what you could carry.

"Not soon enough." Jed set the blade down and reached to the crate for a small oilcloth bundle. He unwrapped it carefully. Four cloudy vials clinked together, their liquid catching the lamplight in sickly milk-green. The stink of it cut through salt and smoke in the room—the kind of sharp that bit inside the nose and left a cold aftertaste.

Brann watched without blinking.

"Don't ask," Jed said. The words came without bite. "It's better if you don't know whether I begged or bought or stole."

Brann shrugged one shoulder. "If you mean to come back, don't come back dead." He stood, crossed the room in two strides that set the floorboards ticking, and set his hand on Jed's shoulder. Usually there'd be weight and humor in that hand, some dockside folly smuggled into the grip. Tonight it was only weight. "Be careful," he said.

Jed nodded once.

Brann let go. He moved to the door, lifted the latch, and paused with it in his fingers. He didn't say anything else. The wind punched the door in when he opened it, rain blowing across the floor. He stepped out, pulling it behind him, and the shack shuddered when the catch set.

Jed sat alone with the storm.

He did not pray. He did not ask the sea. He did the small things he had: checked every knot again; re-oiled the sling pouches; tied a short leather strap around his left forearm where the iron bars might slice; tucked two stones in his cheek to warm them—an old habit from rat-hunting days. He bound the rag-loop to his right palm and tested whether the vial would sit in it without rattling. He cut a square of old sailcloth for the skylight glass so the pieces would fall quiet if he had to break one.

The lamp hissed and guttered low. He pinched it dark. The shack sank into a softer darkness rimmed by flashes at the shutters. Jed pulled his hood up and tied it under his throat. He touched the red thread about his wrist and tightened it until it cut scale. He left the map where it was. He knew it now better than his own scales.

When he opened the door, the storm leaned its weight into him as if it had been waiting for the chance. It made him invisible. It also tried to take him for itself. Cover and hazard both.

He stepped into it and let it wash him cold.

—

Greyhaven under weather was a different city. The dockside—usually a clatter of men shouting over gulls and stink—lay pressed flat, voices rained out of throats. Lanterns bobbed under awnings like weak fish, sputtering. Ropes thrummed hard on masts, and sails, if they weren't already reefed, went mad, snapping and cracking like things trying to break free of their own rigging. Drain spouts vomited water into alleys that had never been meant for rivers. The tide shoved itself up the gut of the harbor and made all the moored ships twitch.

Jed kept to the walls, hugging received rain where the wind didn't scour it. When he crossed open stone he dragged his tail so his steps would sound like vermin, not man or kobold. The storm did most of the work of hiding him, drowning the small clicks of claw on cobble beneath the slap and hiss and rumble.

He lifted his head and tasted the air: tar, rope pitch, fish turned sweet in barrels, the iron bite of lightning not yet fallen. A mouthful of the warrens came back—damp stone, woodsmoke, the way morning almost sounded like tide when you were far enough under rock—and then it went again, swept out by the vinegar stink from the cooper's lane he needed.

He moved.

Watchmen weren't marching tonight so much as tucking themselves out of the weather where they could. He saw two under a stone arch, cloaks pulled tight, heads down. The dog with them stood up against the worst of it, nose up, muzzle tasting what wind came through. Jed slid sideways, into a drain's shadow, and let a sheet of rain fall between him and the animal like a curtain. The dog turned its head the way dogs do when something old in them won't sit still. Its nose twitched toward him. Jed put his cheek against wet stone and breathed through his mouth, slow as counting. A shutter banged hard a street over—some poor bastard hadn't done what Brann had—and the dog flinched and barked at that instead. The watchman swore, slapped the dog's flank, and clung harder to his cloak.

Jed let the thunder roll before he slipped away.

The north-quarter lanes narrowed. Houses leaned toward each other, roofs nearly touching so rain came down in slashes and serpents rather than sheets. He passed the alley where he'd once traded grease for copper; the threshold where a fishwife had called him little rat without venom. The storm made everything honest; even curses sounded like warnings rather than hates.

Left where the lane sagged shallow; again when vinegar bit the back of his tongue. The cooper's shop stood where he knew it would be, shutters shut, a loose hoop rolling and tapping a door someone had forgotten to bring in before the weather hit. Beyond that, a storehouse leaned against the night like a drunk who couldn't quite find his wall. Between them sat the square-shouldered house that mattered.

Two guards at the door. He had drawn them on the map and set them to pacing in his head, but flesh makes a different noise than ink. Their boots made a shallow splash with each turn. Cloaks snapped and clung. Swords hung heavier in storms, scabbards sucking and sticking against wet leather. One smoked, the pipe cupped in both hands to keep it lit. The other blew rain out of his mustache and scowled as if scowls turned weather aside.

Their pacing wasn't perfect—the storm chewed at it, made boots slip, pipes sputter. But through the noise he found the count.

He did not go down. He took the walls.

There's a way you learn to climb when you've spent your first years in damp places. You don't take the obvious chimneys because obvious is where men post archers and where water falls fastest. You don't leap until you've put your hands on the slate and felt whether it means to stay with you or break away. And you don't trust any edge you haven't already hung from.

Jed set his claws into a mortar seam and the other hand to a window jamb. He bled his weight into the wall, felt it answer, then moved a foot and then the other. He made himself smaller than the wind could catch. A gutter overflowed two hands above him—a curtain of water he had to push his face through. It was cold enough to bite eyes and nose. He shut them against it and climbed blind for three breaths until the water let him go.

Halfway up, a slate shifted under his toe and whispered down the roof. He caught a drainpipe in both hands and flattened himself. The slate slid off, hit the street, shattered. The pipe-man guard started and swore and squinted up into the storm. The other turned too slow, rain blinding him. Lightning opened and shut the sky. Jed didn't breathe. The guard wiped his mustache and looked back down. Thunder followed—the sort that ran in your bones. The pipe-man laughed at himself, like men do when they're afraid to name fear, and said something Jed couldn't hear. The other snorted and hitched a knee again; the rhythm resumed.

Jed moved.

The roofline ran him along chimney backs and down to a shoulder of slate that led to the house he wanted. Between this roof and the next was a narrow seam of street that had decided to call itself a canal for the night. He could jump it. In dry weather he wouldn't think about it. Wet makes everything farther and uglier.

He set the rope on the chimney, looped it twice, wedged a short length of dowel—stolen from Brann's net poles—between coil and stone to bite. He gave it a pull. The line bit back. Good. He left a loop around his waist and stood on the last solid slate. The wind shoved him sideways once. He bent his knees and waited for it to finish its thought. When it eased, he counted the guards' paces in his head—two, three, turn, pause—then ran three quick steps and went out and away.

For a moment he was a thing the storm had a right to, weight picked up by wind and held over black. His claws hit slate on the other side and skated. His tail whipped the wrong way and corrected. He dropped to his belly and felt the rope take the last of the slide. A sound escaped him, half laugh, half choke—not joy, not anything human. The storm ate it before even he could hear it whole.

126

He pulled the rope to him, slacked it free from the chimney, and coiled it snake-tight as he went. The skylight waited ahead, square in the center of the roof like an eye. Rain sluiced off its glass panes and spit into the gutter. Iron lay over it like a cage, four bars each way, rust tracing the metal a scab's color where paint had given up some storm long before this one.

Jed went flat and slid to the frame, testing every slate with the edge of his hand. One cracked; he eased weight off it and felt it hold out of stubbornness. He came up on the windward side and made himself a shadow smaller than the bars.

Below the glass, a room glowed low and dim. Not fire-bright; not tavern-yellow. The kind of light a lamp gives when a man trims it down to sleepy. Jed squinted and let the watery reflection wiggle back into the room. A table. A chair. Another door thrown half-open to darker hall beyond. Rain blurred everything else.

He lay there and watched.

The guards turned. Ten paces. Turn. Rough but countable. Street: empty save for water running like ropes laid side by side. Room: lamplow and shadow—and that pelt like a wound dragged across a back for a blink where the light caught and moved.

His mouth had gone dry. He swallowed rain. It tasted of iron and rope and slate. Good. Those were this city's flavors, and he would use the city to cut its monster.

He measured the bars in his head. If he poured at the crosspoints first, the frame would cradle what gave and keep the cut pieces from falling through and sounding an alarm. If he poured mid-bar, the weight might drop and ring like a bell. The corners would be strongest. He would start two in from the edge, where rust sat thick and wet. He would wrap a fold of sailcloth around the cut before it let go so it wouldn't clink against cage or glass. He set the cloth under his chin, ready to flick it into place with two fingers while the acid ate.

He breathed once, slow. Thunder rolled. Wind lunged. The guards turned.

Jed lifted the vial.

He eased the cork with his teeth, kept it in his mouth so the storm wouldn't steal it and so he wouldn't be left scrambling with glass in one hand and teeth in the other. The reek of the acid hit the roof and fought the rain a moment, sharp enough to cut under the sky's wet. He set the lip of the vial to iron, found the rust's soft place with it, and did not yet tilt.

Lightning opened the world. The bars flashed wet. Below, something moved—someone shifting on a chair, or a boot catching the table leg as a man stood. Jed held. The light closed. The thunder that followed took a heartbeat, maybe two, maybe ten.

He set the sailcloth where it needed to be. He set his other hand to brace against slate made slick by a city's worth of weather and sins. He found the timing of the guards in his chest and made their crooked paces his count.

He waited for the sky to break.

And when it did—when thunder came big enough to shake knives in drawers three houses over—Jed let the first drop fall.

He did not pour. He let that single bead kiss iron and tell him how fast it would eat, how loud it would hiss, how much the rain would dull it, how many breaths he would have before hard went bone-soft.

The hiss rose—sharp, burning—a snake under the storm.

Jed held between breath and heartbeat, the next thunderclap coiled above him.

He had never been more careful, and never closer to coming apart. The storm asked him to let go. He held, teeth bared.

He watched the iron smoke under the drop.

He waited for the next roll of thunder.

He lowered the vial a fraction more.

And stopped.

Chapter 25

The Captain in Chains

The iron had gone soft enough to lie.

Jed pressed the folded sailcloth to the crosspiece, braced on his forearms, and leaned until his shoulders shook. The bar sagged with a wet rasp, the rain trying to hold it whole even as the acid ate it hollow. He felt metal give the way old bone gives—reluctant, then suddenly. He caught the falling piece in the cloth before it could kiss the glass, eased it aside, and set his weight to the next.

Thunder chewed at the edges of the world. Beneath it, the hiss of acid was a snake under the rain.

He worked crosspoints first. Let the frame keep its pride while his cloth and hands did the talking. Piece by quiet piece, the cage became a story of gaps: one rib eaten thin, another folded, another softened to the softness of meat. When the last segment bent with a tired sigh, he breathed once through his teeth, took the lamp-dulled measure of the room below—door left, table beneath the skylight, cot along the right wall—and slid through the hole he had made.

The chamber smelled of wine, lamp smoke, wet wool—the stink of a man certain his roof would keep the sky out. A low lamp guttered on the table, its trimmed wick throwing a stale yellow over coins, half-rolled maps, a plate with a rind of cheese gone slick. Rushes muffled the floorboards under Jed's pads. In the near left corner, a guard slept crooked in a chair, chin propped and listing, breath bubbling with drink. The only door stood to Jed's left, its latch on his side; someone had kicked the spare chair under it as a brace.

Jed wanted quiet. He took it.

He eased the sling from his belt, fitted a stone to the pouch. The cords purred through his fingers once—habit—then he pinched the leather throat and snapped the stone with a short, tight wrist. It struck the guard beneath the ear. A small, wet sound; a bellows that had been working too hard suddenly forgot how. The man sagged sideways with the chair. Jed was across the floor before wood scraped. Knife already in hand, he cut clean and deep. Warmth spilled, steam sweet in the lamp's old light. The snore ended as if someone had set a palm over its mouth.

He wiped the blade on the dead man's cloak without looking at the face. Faces had a way of not leaving.

Beyond the table: a cot shoved against the far wall beneath the right-hand shutter. A heavy shape lay there, boots still on, wolf pelt thrown over shoulders like a private flag. The hair of it was matted at the collar from old smoke and newer rain. Jed could see the line of a scabbard; the belt unbuckled but not forgotten; the jaw he remembered from the warrens as clearly as smoke.

He moved the way a shadow does when a door opens.

His weight went onto the cot, right knee into sternum through pelt; left foot planted on the floorboards for drive; knife to throat, the edge dimpling flesh. He kept his voice low—the kind of whisper made for one ear and no others.

"Do you remember the warrens?"

Steel kissed skin. Blood rose in a thin line, a glossed red smile where Jed would never see one again.

Veynar's eyes opened as if someone had cut them into the world. No fog. No crawl back from dreams. Only recognition, hardening into something crueler.

"Ah," he breathed. His right hand shot up and closed around Jed's knife wrist with a speed that cheated size and drink. Fingers locked scale against bone. His left hand hunted his belt for steel.

Jed stabbed down left-handed, under the seam where pelt met flesh. The blade sank into the meaty right shoulder—the one that drove the sword. Veynar roared and rolled, all weight and violence. The world flipped; Jed's back hit the table edge ribs-first—white burst, copper taste—coins skittering, maps tearing. The lamp rocked, slopped oil, caught again. Veynar's boot came down where Jed's head had been; the plank split under the miss.

"UP!" Veynar bellowed. The sound raked down the stairs and through the house. "To me! Now!"

Boots below; the ring and scrape of men grabbing what they should have had in hand already. Jed planted feet and came off the floor before the next stamp could pin him to it.

Veynar moved to meet him—slower for the shoulder wound, but not slow. Sword half out in the left hand now. Jed cut across the right thigh high and quick; tendon bit through with a sound that would find him again in sleep. Veynar's leg buckled, then braced, body remembering how to be a weapon even as parts of it failed. His blade bit air, then bit a chair and split it. Jed darted left and chopped at the outside of the left knee. Veynar pivoted and backhanded him across the mouth. Jed hit the wall and tasted the iron that was his.

"Rat," Veynar said, breath serrated. "Vermin. It was business before, now it's personal."

He came with the blade now, owning the center of the small room—door to Jed's left, cot to his right, table between. Big men are larger when they decide a space and a sword both belong to them. Jed slid the table into the lane. The sword punched through the tabletop and the lamp with it. Oil went. Flame climbed the grain with greedy fingers. The light slid orange along steel. Smoke bloomed, slowly, then less slowly. For an instant both were shadow cut by new fire.

Jed kicked a map roll into flame and kicked the flaming roll into Veynar's thighs. The man swore; he batted it away with the flat; he stepped wrong on his bad leg and turned the stumble into a lunge because that is what men like him do—turn even failing into direction.

The door latch rattled. A fist tried it. "Captain!" a voice, high with the kind of fear that makes knives clumsy. The chair brace held. Bless the sleeping guard's laziness.

Jed jumped to the table, springing past a cut, and landed on the cot. The cot collapsed. The room slanted. Veynar took the last step with his weight on the wrong leg, fell into Jed instead of past him, and the two of them went to the floor in a knot the rushes did nothing to forgive.

Then it was hands.

Jed drove the knife where knives make final arguments. Veynar turned ribs into shields and took them through meat. He roared and hooked an arm under Jed the way a fisherman hooks what he means to eat later. Jed lifted and slammed into the bedpost; something cracked—wood or rib; hiss in his ears that wasn't stormy. A hot band cinched his left side and did not let go.

Hands came to his throat.

He brought the sling up into that. Cord loops found themselves like old habits do. He dropped it behind Veynar's neck, crossed the forearms, and hauled, turning his whole back into rope. The world narrowed to the hard fact of cutting breath. Veynar took Jed in both fists and pinned him to the wall like a problem. Hammered him—head to wood, spine to plaster, once, twice, again—trying to turn the house into a weapon. Jed's forearms went numb; his fingers stayed knotted white in cords out of spite.

"CAPTAIN!" from the far side of the door. The latch shrieked; the brace groaned.

Veynar got two fingers under the cord, tore skin to find a purchase, found it. The line slipped a finger's thickness. Jed jammed his knuckles into the gap, making new pain so the old wouldn't win, and bit the forearm that fumbled for air. Tendon rolled under his molars; blood filled his mouth hot and high.

Veynar let go of the cord to hit him. Fist, forearm, elbow—Jed learned the map of the blows the way he had learned the map of the streets: left to temple, right to ear, shoulder to mouth. When the elbow dropped, he rolled with it, came up under the arm, and stabbed where breath lives beside the hip. He drove until his knuckles kissed skin. Veynar gasped and made a noise. No captain let his men hear twice. Weight bowed. Jed ripped the blade sideways, then back. The rushes drank like they had been thirsty.

The door screamed. Wood split. A knife blade snaked through the gap, tasting air. "Hold!" someone shouted, too many boots behind to fit in a room this small.

Jed didn't have a "hold." He had "finish" and "die."

He let the sling go and went back to the knife.

Veynar's sword arm shook now. The shoulder no longer understood the orders it gave itself. Thigh flooded boot. He still came on, panting, smiling a smile that had no business in a mouth this wet with blood. He feinted low once—testing whether Jed was a thing that could still be fooled. Jed didn't bite. He waited like a gull watches for wind to change. When the blade turned heavy and late, he slid inside it and opened the left forearm from wrist to meat, drawing a second mouth. Veynar swore and punched; Jed took the punch on the skull, light-burst, room sideways. He stabbed at breathing and hit rib—hard, skidding.

Inventory, fast: left side bad—two ribs gone to liars; breath a bellows with a crack; right hand slick; jaw ringing; vision arguing which room to show. Heat running under his cloak at the left flank: not lamp oil. Him.

Veynar came through the ruin like weather. He swung; overbalanced; caught the post; used everything that was left because that was the training in him: make even failing into force. Jed let him come, then stepped where the man needed him not to be.

He looped the sling again—quick and filthy—and wrenched backward, peg jaw up. The chin lifted. Jed drove the knife not at the throat this time, but up under the jaw's hinge, the soft seam behind the bone where the tongue's root hides and the big vessels rise. Steel slid into heat; the knife shocked his hand with the beat of blood. He felt it—pulse to metal to wrist, a drum he would never forget.

Veynar's hands found Jed's wrists. Jed kicked the good knee as you kick a door someone holds shut. It went. They fell together, cord in one hand, knife in the other, rain and fire and breath all too loud.

They hit the floor. Jed landed on top by accident and made it look like design. He planted a knee on Veynar's sternum where ribs hate weight and leaned until the breath stopped arguing. The cord cut; the knife held its place under the jaw, and with a short, cruel pull, he widened the wound. Warmth came out in ropey surges, bright even in bad light. It sprayed the underside of the cot; it turned the wolf pelt black; it painted Jed's forearms scarlet and hot. Veynar's boots drummed the floorboards for a count; his fingers scrabbled at Jed's wrist, then slipped, then slowed.

The door gave another inch. A hand shoved through; someone screamed a name that didn't help. "Captain! Captain!"

Jed's weight stayed where it was. He watched the eyes because eyes tell truth first. They had been bright with hate; they went glassy in a breath, then a breath and a half. The pupils swam, then spread; the lids trembled without closing. The chest bucked once under Jed's knee—an ugly, last will of muscle—and then it didn't. The pulse in the knife stilled. The spray softened to a pour, the pour to a leak, the leak to nothing but warmth making cold where it had no business.

Veynar Blackfang died with a cord at his throat and a kobold's knee on his ribs.

Jed stayed long enough to be certain. He knew death in a way that never leaves a body once it has learned it. The quiet arrived—the particular quiet a room finds when the largest thing in it stops insisting it exists. The weight under his knee changed to unarguing weight. He put two fingers to the neck he'd opened for proof he did not need. There was no proof left to give.

The door crashed another hand's width. A sword point stabbed through, withdrew, stabbed again like a beak. "Captain—" a voice broke on the word.

Jed had heartbeats left and work still to spend them on.

He drew the knife from under the jaw, flipped it in his fingers, and with those same two clean, unlovely strokes—down and across—he cut his clan's sign into Veynar's cheek. Not show. Not flourish. Record. Blood ran into hair and mouth; the mark sat red and certain on a face that had smiled over smoke.

"This is for mine," he said. Not loud. Not for the door. For the dead that still answered to him.

He pushed off, wiped the blade once on fur because habit still lives even in holy moments, and jammed the broken chair deeper under the latch with his shoulder. The brace shrieked and settled. It would not keep men out. It would make them slower. That was all he needed.

The skylight's black was a square above, rimmed in rain. He took two steps and a jump, caught the frame with elbows, ribs shrieking white where the table had kissed them, kicked into the gap he had made in the bars, and wriggled through with a sound like splitting fruit. The glass licked his back cold. The storm slapped his face clean and blessed.

"Roof!" someone below. Then the door finally tore wide and hit the wall with a bang that rattled window frames. Men poured in over a floor slick with their captain. One gagged. Another swore until he ran out of the good words. "Up!" a third barked—a sergeant's voice, iron trying to remember itself. "Up—go!"

Jed didn't wait to be made a lesson.

Slate wanted him dead. He went low and kept weight close to stone, rope looped over shoulder like a clinging thing. Lightning opened the world in white ribs. For one breath he saw everything: the cooper's hoop still tapping; the storehouse leaning like a drunk with his friend gone; the guards at the front door looking up as if rain had suddenly become news; the street gone river; the harbor making all its ships shiver.

A quarrel hissed up through the hole and took the air next to his skull with the sound of a sharp inhale; it went off into the night to hit some gutter that would complain later. He rolled right; his left ribs flared so hot the world pinwheeled; bile and blood climbed his throat. He swallowed both and kept moving.

He reached the gap he had crossed before. The rope was already in his hand—the hand remembered for the hand that would need it. He flicked it around a chimney, let it bite. The wind lunged; he waited, counted its temper, and went when a gust was breath and not a shove. He jumped, weight tight and low, tail cutting his balance the way boys had mocked when boys were the biggest thing he had to fear. He landed in a crouch, the right knee taking it hard; the joint flared and tried to fold. He rode the slide on forearms and belly until slate held. The rope caught the last of him. He lay flat a heartbeat, cheek to wet stone, and felt warmth leaving his left flank steady as a leak. When he lifted, his palm left a blood print.

He slacked the line, dragged it free, and coiled as he crawled. Behind him: "Ladder!" "Street!" "Cut him off!" Too many orders for too much wet.

135

He ran a low crouch, weight forward. Each step jabbed a nail under the cracked ribs. The sword stripe across those same ribs had reopened the night's older hurt; wet seeped and stuck the cloak to his side. His mouth tasted iron and brine; when he spat, it made pink ropes on the slate. Rope burns scored his wrists where the sling had paid for its work; the jaw throbbed with a rising egg.

A squad of Watch turned into the lane ahead, shields up, hoods making men into shapes. The dog with them caught motion above and barked twice, ugly and certain. Jed slid behind a chimney and made himself nothing until lightning handled the introductions. When it struck, it struck hard enough to make the dog swallow its bark. The flash made bright day for a blink. By the time night returned, Jed had ghosted along a seam to the next roof. "There!" a watchman pointed, too late and too wet.

He took a slanting run on purpose, let the rain make the slate a river, rode it to a low parapet, used it as a ramp and flew. He hit the next roof bad—right knee again, light sparking in his head—and rolled with it. A tile broke and clattered into the lane. A man below swore the way men swear when roofs participate in weather.

His left side wobbled, heat and needle. Breath rasped high; when he coughed it put a red thread on his tongue. He pressed his left forearm tight to the ribs as he moved; the pressure made his vision swim but bought a little breath that didn't spear. His right hand kept checking belt and knife—counting what still lived with him—without asking permission.

Another gap; smaller. No time for a second anchor. He went flat and long, tail carving balance. He landed crooked, stayed on his knees a heartbeat because the world had decided to tilt, then crawled until legs remembered their work.

The roofs fell away toward water. Dock breath in his nose. He made for darker eaves and gutters where footsteps drown themselves. Behind him the city howled—battered orders, three different angers, a bell that meant confusion first and command second.

He did not go straight to the shack. The city was not finished with the night.

He cut a crooked path through rafters and gutters and slates until he could come down where footsteps drowned themselves: behind a row of barrels in the yard of a shuttered cooper; into a runnel slick with stinking water. He set his feet where the rain was loudest and waited while a dog slid on tiles and a handler cursed it away. Men shouted in three angers: those who had lost a captain, those who had to answer for losing a captain, and those who had merely wanted sleep. Bells started and failed and started again. Somewhere a woman upended a basin of water and cried when it turned out to be blood she poured.

Jed waited until the first rush of stupidity ran its course. A man once told him storms obey their own count: first the fools, then the brave, then the clever. The clever were only just now getting out of bed.

He eased into the alleys. The storm leaned on him, found purchase in his cloak and tried to set him backward; he set his head forward and walked through it. He crossed a lane where the river had come up to talk to the city and left the conversation unfinished. He ducked a rope line the wind had torn from a pulley. He slid his small body through a fence gap the way he had learned to slide himself through tighter, darker spaces that smelled of home and smoke and love.

By the time the shack took shape as something more than black on black, the rain had gone from hammer to nails to steady pins. The ropes in the rafters were singing, the kind of tight hum that says a knot was tied right and will spite the weather another hour. The tied shutter was still a tied shutter. The door's latch kissed his palm the way a friend does when a friend is wood and iron.

He went inside and shut the storm out to a murmur.

He stood with his back to the door, breathing, letting the room come back into a room. He set the knife on the crate. The map lay where he had left it, its corner torn where claws had lost their patience. He took the torn corner and pressed it against the rest as if that would mend anything.

Then he looked down at his hands. The blood had started to dry into rivers that would crack if he moved wrong. He worked his fingers anyway, counting them as if the number had any chance of changing. His wrists were raw where the cord had bit; his right kneecap sang complaint; the left side of his shirt clung to him with warmth gone cool.

He did not speak. To speak would make it something else.

He reached for the bucket, tipped it, and hissed when cold took hot from his arms. Red ran to the floor in pink sheets then thin. He scrubbed until steel and scale looked like themselves. He left the water the color of remembering. When he bent, his ribs ticked—cracked boards in a hull.

The rope around his wrist had gone slack. He pulled it tight until it bit, as if it had been slacking while he worked. He tore a strip from old sailcloth, wrapped it around his ribs twice, and hauled it tight until the room narrowed and then came back. He tied it with teeth and a sound he kept in his throat.

Veynar's eyes were a problem that would not return.

He stood a long time, listening for a step that was not weather. When his own breath stopped sounding like someone else's, he crossed to the stove, set two bits of half-dry kindling he'd laid aside, and coaxed a small honesty from a spark. He sat on the floor and put his back to the stove, heat biting through wet cloth until it hurt in a way he could name.

He did not know if the storm meant to hold another day. He did not know if the Watch would find the bars, taste the acid in their tongues, put line to line with the old sailors' brawl and the smell of blackgut on the night the hall burned. He did not know if the wolves would fight over the headless pack or if the city would decide to love some other monster tomorrow.

But he knew this: the rope had been cut.

If there were a cost yet, he would pay it standing up. He had the hands for that now, even if one of them shook and every breath clicked like a cracked rib.

The stove breathed. The storm breathed back. Somewhere in the city, the bells chose one story over another and sang it for men who wanted songs.

Jed sat with the knife where it lived. He did not sleep. He did not pray.

He waited for the tide to turn.

Chapter 26

Salt That Stays

They were waiting with their bags packed, two shadows hunched by the shack's thin fire. Wind worried the door until Jed shouldered it open. He took one step inside, another, and the room tipped under him.

Mara came up out of her chair like a thrown knife. Brann's hands were already out, catching Jed under the arms before he hit the floorboards.

Jed lifted his head enough to find their faces—both tight with fear, both trying not to be. He bared his teeth in something that wanted to be a grin.

"It is done," he said.

Then the dark found him and took him whole.

—

He woke to the smell of broth and pitch and clean thread.

The world arranged itself slowly: roof boards patched with tar; the knotted line of Brann's cot frame under his shoulder blades; linen wound hard around his ribs. His skin smelled faintly of sea salt and something bitter that bit like crushed herbs. A neat little ladder of stitches tugged at his flank with each breath.

Mara dozed in a chair, arms folded, cheek pillowed on her bicep, mouth slightly open in a soft snore she'd deny until her dying day. A basket sat at her feet like a guard dog—cloth, needles, a spool of waxed gut, a small pot of salve with its lid off. The bandages on Jed's side were straight as dock planks.

139

In the next room, a spoon rang the lip of a pot. Brann hummed a nothing tune, off-key.

Jed shifted. Pain bit. He sucked air through his teeth.

Mara's eyes snapped open. "Don't you go moving and tear my stitches, you daft fool." Her voice was sleep-rough and all business. She flicked a glance toward the doorway. "Brann. He's awake. Bring him something before he eats his own tail."

Brann came in with a chipped mug steaming in his big hands. "Storms and saints." He held the mug under Jed's nose. "Well, you don't do things halfway, I'll give you that." He eased an arm behind Jed's shoulders, lifting him just enough to drink. "Sip, scales. Let it sit."

The broth tasted of bones and onion, warm as a hand on a cold back. It shook in the mug when Jed's claws trembled; Brann steadied both mug and hand without comment.

"How long?" Jed rasped.

"Two days," Mara said, already peering at her work like she expected the thread to jump out of his skin in rebellion. "You slept like a rock. That wasn't praise."

"We took turns breathing at you," Brann added—too light and too serious at once. "Watch knocked twice. I told them I snore. They believed me. Mara told them if they dragged a sick cousin out of her house she'd bite every last finger off 'em and make stew. They believed her more."

Mara sniffed. "They poked around, asked after a kobold. I told them I've got enough vermin in my flour without harboring more. They looked at the sacks and decided I was the sort to bite. They're not wrong." She sat back, studying Jed's face. "Greyhaven's buzzing, you should know. Men running their tongues raw. Some say the Wolf is dead. Some swear he wasn't ever a wolf, only a drunk in a pelt. Some talk about a rat with a knife that writes on people." Her mouth tightened. "Your... mark."

Jed set the empty mug on his chest and closed his eyes. Veynar's blood had been hot. The sound of it on the floor had been louder than he liked to remember. He had cut the sign quick into the man's cheek—two clean strokes through a line—and then the room had turned red and narrow.

140

"Let them talk," he said. His voice came out small and even. "Let it spread."

"It has," Brann said. "Across the quay, up Fishers' Row, all the way to Barrel Street. Children were chalking the sign on walls this morning. The Watch scraped it off by noon. They chalked it again by dusk."

A muscle jumped along Jed's jaw. He was too tired to smile, too tired to show whatever lived beside it.

Mara's hand hovered, not quite touching his brow. "The guildhall—" She stopped herself, made a small noise of irritation at her own softening. "No one can tie that to us now. The Wolf's boys have bigger problems—missing coin, missing captain, missing faces. We don't have to leave. Not today." Her gaze sharpened. "You hear me? Brann and I are staying."

Brann nodded, heavy and certain. "Shack's ours. Oven's hers. Docks will always be docks. Let wolves chew on their shame."

Jed breathed slowly, feeling the bandages pull and settle. The relief in him ached as badly as the wounds. "Good," he said. "Then I can say it. I won't be staying."

Mara's eyes went to flint. "You most definitely will, until I say you can walk without leaking."

"I'll heal," Jed said. "Then I'll go."

Brann's grin slid off his face and came back smaller. "Watch is beating the alleys for a kobold. You'll stand out like a bright coin. The shack's quiet. We can keep you hidden a while yet."

"I won't hide forever," Jed said. "I like your walls. I like your food. I like... this." He didn't have a better word than the small room and the broth and Mara's neat stitches and Brann's big hands steadying a mug. "But if I stay, I make your lives small as my hole under a boat. I can't ask that. And I can't sit in a room for the rest of my days, waiting for a knock."

Mara's mouth went through several shapes, none of them kind. At last she huffed through her nose. "Don't think telling me the truth makes me less angry."

"It's not at you," Jed said. "It's the world. And me."

Brann set the mug aside. "Then we do this my way, just for a handful of days. You eat like you've got a future. You sleep like a man who didn't try to take on a beast with a butter knife. You let Mara growl and stitch. And when you can stand

141

up without swaying like a drunk on a deck, we'll talk about your bloody noble exit. Agreed?"

Jed watched the boards for a few breaths. The shack smelled like tar and soup and clean cloth. The tide beyond the pilings breathed in time with him. "Agreed."

"Good." Brann clapped his hands once. "And don't you dare laugh. It'll hurt. Then I'll laugh at you."

Jed's tail twitched despite himself. "That seems unfair."

"Life is." Brann's grin came back full. "But there's stew."

Mara rose, the chair scraping. She flicked Jed's ear, gentle only by accident. "Sleep. If you tear a stitch I'll sew you shut so tight you'll squeak when you breathe."

"Already do," Jed murmured, eyes closing, the corner of his mouth almost remembering. "Ask Brann."

Brann snorted. "He squeaks. Like a very angry kettle."

Jed's laugh surprised him and punished him in the same breath. Pain lanced across his ribs so sharp his eyes watered. He hissed and curled on instinct.

Mara was on him in an instant, tutting like a gull pecking a boat's seam. "What did I just tell you? No laughing. Saints preserve me from fools and men."

"I'm a kobold," Jed said, breathless, eyes watering. "Half credit."

Mara's mouth fought a losing battle with a smile. "Sleep before I feed you to the nets."

He slept.

Chapter 27

Moving On

The city rattled like a bucket of shells the next three days.

Watchmen knocked at the shack twice more; Brann filled the doorway with shoulders and easy talk until they decided their time was better spent shouting at men who ran. A Blackfang with a bandage on his ear came once with a friend, both ugly with loss. Mara stood behind the counter with a cleaver in view and said, very politely, that if they bled on her floor she'd make them mop it with their tongues. They left wiping their boots on the step like scolded schoolboys.

Rumor worked as hard as any fishwife. The Rat-Dragon left marks, they said—scars on faces, signs on walls. He was a spirit, he was a man, he was a kobold with a knife; he was three children in a cloak. He was the story you told a drunk to make him piss in a different alley. He was the whisper that turned the bravest head when a gull cried at night.

Jed healed because Mara made him and because Brann would not let him do otherwise. He ate broth and then bread and then an egg boiled so perfect he would have wept if he'd had tears left for such things. He slept until sleep turned from a dark hole into a soft room. He changed his own bandages under Mara's glare. He walked from cot to door, door to stove, stove to door again, learning where the pain had moved today.

By the third morning his steps were steady. By the fourth he could roll his shoulder without feeling the cut pull. By the fifth, Mara prodded the stitches and grunted, which from Mara was halfway to applause.

Brann brought him a little pack—a coil of thin line, a whetstone, a tin cup that had seen enough fires to look like charcoal. "For the road," he said, eyes studiously not on Jed's face. "And a little flesh for the bones when the bones forget they're covered." He set a wrapped parcel on the table: smoked fish and a heel of bread, heavy as stone. "Don't be noble and refuse it. I'll throw it at your head and Mara will have to stitch you again."

Mara, at the stove, didn't turn. "I will not."

"You absolutely will," Brann said cheerfully.

Jed closed the parcel. His claws hesitated on the string. "I don't..." He made a vague gesture that meant everything he couldn't fit into words. "I can't say it right."

"Then don't," Mara said. She turned, wiped her hands on her apron, and stepped into his space to fix his collar, which did not need fixing. Her fingers were quick and surprisingly gentle. "You'll write if you find a place that doesn't stink of wolves." She put a small glass vial in his palm and closed his fingers over it. "Acid. For bars. Or stubborn locks. Or fish scales. Don't waste it."

Jed looked down at it. "You're trying to get rid of me faster."

"Obviously." Her mouth twitched. "Before I start liking you." Her voice snagged sharp again, then cracked on the edge of something she refused to call pleading. "And if you die out there, I'll know it, Jed. I'll know it, and I'll never forgive you for wasting what we've kept alive here."

Brann cleared his throat and looked everywhere but at them. Then he stopped pretending and hauled Jed into his arms with a careful squeeze that avoided the worst of the stitches. "Little brother," he said into Jed's frill. "Keep your head down, your claws sharp, and your boots where your feet are."

Jed patted the man's shoulder twice in a gesture he'd seen humans use when they meant something and were afraid to say it. "You laugh too loudly," he said. "And your stew is too salty."

Brann sniffed. "Lies."

"True," Mara said.

Jed settled the pack on his shoulders. The shack felt smaller all at once, as if his body had learned its edges by heart and was already missing them. He looked once at the low table with its burn mark like a map of a country he'd learned to navigate, at the cot's sag where his weight had been, at the little basket with thread and needle that would smell like him until the sea took the smell away.

"I'll be back if I can," he said, which was true and not a promise.

"Mind the Watch," Mara said, lifting her chin.

"Mind the wolves," Brann said.

Jed stepped into the doorway. The tide was just turning, the flats shining like skin under a sheen of oil. Gulls argued with themselves. The city breathed smoke and gossip. He breathed with it and went.

He walked the coast. The wind had teeth. Salt got into the cut in his side and nagged it into honesty. He kept the line of water on his right shoulder and the low dunes on his left and let the city fall behind. Its voice dropped to a hum, then to nothing. Sand found its way into his boots. He let it.

He thought of where he would go and did not decide. South, maybe. There were whispers of warrens tucked into cliffs two days down the coast—small as pockets, mean as splinters, but alive. Or farther yet, to a place where men counted coin without counting the scales of the hand that took it. He would see.

He stopped where the skiff had once been. Storms and men had finished what the Watch had not—boards scattered like the bones of a fish left too long in sun. The patch of sand where his lair had hunched was only a darker kiss on the beach now, shaped by memory more than wind.

He stood a long time, hands at his sides, listening to the careful noise the sea makes when it doesn't want to bother anyone. The gulls wheeled. The water heaved. In the sound he almost heard voices—Brann cursing a card hand, Mara muttering over a split seam, Yarra singing to Kep when the warrens were still whole.

Then he crouched and dug in his pouch. The little stone lay where it always had—a smooth oval, thumb-warm from a hundred nights, his clan's mark scratched into it with Yarra's knife long ago: one line, two short strokes through.

He had pressed it into wet sand a hundred times, into soot, into the soft wood under the skiff's ribs. He had kept it because he had not known how to move without it.

He put the stone to his mouth and touched it to his teeth. He tasted salt and the old oil of his own hands. He held it a breath longer.

"Yarra," he said. "Kep."

He stood and threw.

The stone arced out, a small bright thing against a flat gray day, and went into the water without a sound he could hear. The rings it left spread a little, then were nothing, then were everything.

Jed watched the place where it had gone until the tide rubbed the spot smooth. Then he tucked his hands into his cloak, turned south, and started walking.

The coast gave him its weather and its silence. His steps cut their own sign into the damp sand—a line with two short cuts through, there and gone and there again with each new tide. The mark lived and was erased, lived and was erased, as if the sea itself were keeping pace.

Behind him, Greyhaven exhaled. Its rumors would knot and spread, its alleys would fill with chalk marks, its Watch would scrape and scrape again. What he had carved into its night would take a long time to fade.

He did not look back. He did not hurry. He carried Brann's laugh, Mara's sharpness, Yarra's voice, Kep's heel in his palm. Salt stayed in his wounds, in his scales, in his breath.

Salt that stayed, and a road that waited.

Also by

About the author

Daniel Sheley has been telling stories for most of his life, shaped early by myth, folklore, and writers such as Thomas Malory and William Shakespeare. Those influences, combined with lived experience, inform his focus on character, belief, and the cost of choice.He served in the U.S. Navy in both technical and leadership roles, experiences that deepened his understanding of systems, pressure, and human behavior. He is the award-winning author of Heartcoil, Lux Mendacium, and For Scales Alone (2026 Indies Today Awards - 2nd Runner-Up in Urban Fantasy). His forthcoming novel, The Soul-Sung, was a finalist in the Writers' League of Texas Manuscript Contest and launches The Vaeritas Saga.Daniel lives in Midland, Texas, with his wife and blended family and continues to explore the space where myth, memory, and meaning meet through his fiction.

www.ingramcontent.com/pod-product-compliance
Lightning Source LLC
Chambersburg PA
CBHW050452110726
47899CB00003B/916